THE AUTHOR

Billy Bob Buttons is a young talented author. On top of being a secondary school English teacher, he is also a pilot.

Born in the Viking city of York, he and his wife, Therese, a true Swedish girl from the IKEA county of Småland, now live in Stockholm and London. Their twin girls, Rebecca and Beatrix, and little boy, Albert, inspire Billy Bob every day to pick up a pen and work on his books.

When not writing, he enjoys tennis and playing 'MONSTER!' with his three children.

He is the author of the much loved, The Gullfoss Legends, Rubery Award finalist, Felicity Brady and the Wizard's Bookshop, TOR Assassin Hunter, TOR Wolf Rising, TIFFANY SPARROW Spook Slayer, Muffin Monster and The Boy Who Piddled In His Grandad's Slippers..

I Think I Murdered Miss was his ninth children's novel and won the UK People's Book Prize.

BILLY BOB BUTTONS' BOOKS

FELICITY BRADY AND THE WIZARD'S BOOKSHOP

GALIBRATH'S WILL
ARTICULUS QUEST
INCANTUS GOTHMOG
GLUMWEEDY'S DEVIL
CROWL'S CREEPERS

THE GULLFOSS LEGENDS

I THINK I MURDERED MISS

TOR
ASSASSIN HUNTER

TOR
WOLF RISING

MUFFIN MONSTER

TIFFANY SPARROW
SPOOK SLAYER

THE BOY WHO PIDDLED IN HIS GRANDAD'S SLIPPERS

Felicity Brady and the Wizard's Bookshop

Billy Bob Button:

book 1
GALIBRATH'S WILL

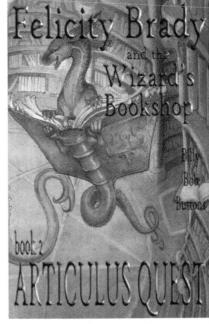

Felicity Brady and the Wizard's Bookshop

Billy Bob Buttons

book 2
ARTICULUS QUEST

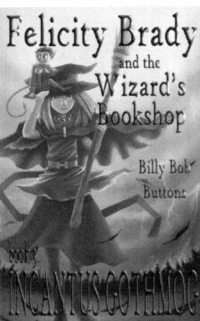

Felicity Brady and the Wizard's Bookshop

Billy Bob Buttons

book 3
INCANTUS GOTHMOG

'Muffins and a big, hungry ...the perfect children's book recipe.
Kids' Zo..

FROM THE
AWARD-WINNING,
BEST-SELLING

Muffin MONSTER

Billy Bob Buttons

Remember:
...en you hunt assassins
...trust nobody.

TOR
ASSASSIN HUNTER

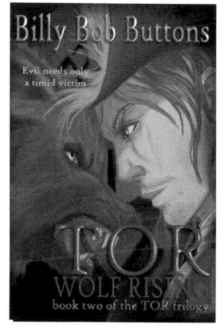

Billy Bob Buttons

Evil needs only
a timid victim

TOR
WOLF RISING
book two of the TOR trilogy

by award-winning author
Billy Bob Buttons

The gripping story
of a magical legend

the
GULLY
legends

BILLY BOB BUTTONS

TIFFANY SPARROW
SPOOK SLAYER

THE WISHING SHELF PRESS

Published by THE WISHING SHELF PRESS, UK.
ISBN 978 1522791072
www.bbbuttons.co.uk
Edited by Alison Emery, Therese Råsbäck and Svante Jurnell.
Cover by Sarah Boxall. www.little-miss-boxie.com
Page 72. Quote from Star Trek II, The Wrath of Khan, Paramount Pics, 1982.

For Saleem and his wonderful family

NOTE

Simon, the hero of this book, has Asperger's syndrome. It is when a person finds it difficult to tell others what they need and how they feel. They also find it difficult to know how others feel and what is the 'normal' thing to do. Often, but not always, a person with Asperger's can be very, very clever and can have overly-strong interests. Simon, for example, is obsessed by Star Trek. Both children and adults can suffer from it.

Interested in Asperger's syndrome?
www.autism.org.uk

YESTERDAY

Chapter 1

A BIG SCARY NOTHINGNESS

MY NAME IS SIMON SPITTLE AND I THINK - NO, I know, I murdered Miss Belcher. I don't carry a gun. Or a knife. Or even a toothpick, but yesterday, in French, I wished for her to be run over by a bus and, later that very day, she was. A big, red double-decker with yellow wheels and a picture of a clown on the bonnet. A Billy Smart's Circus bus.

I did not see it happen but Isabella did and she told me Miss left this world with an almighty 'SPLAT!' Up to sixty percent of a human body is water so I think 'SPLAT!' is probably correct.

My problem is, I don't like French. Or German. Or Spanish. Or even English. They upset me. The teachers tell me a rule; tell me how important it is to follow the rule, then they tell me when NOT to follow the rule. 'I before e,' they say. 'Jot this down in your book, Simon. I before e.' Then they say, 'Except.' 'Except after c,' they say. The word 'Except' exists simply to bewilder, puzzle and perplex. 'Except' upsets me terribly along with 'but', 'however', 'nevertheless' and 'willy-nilly'.

I like maths. And physics. And chemistry.

I Think I Murdered Miss

$1+1=2$, $E=mc^2$, drop a spoonful of nitro-glycerine ($H_3H_5N_3O_9$) on the floor and it will always, ALWAYS blow your foot off. No excepts, no buts, no howevers and no willy-nilliness. Even history is OK. Lots of facts in history. The Battle of Hastings was in 1066. Thomas Crapper invented the loo. End of story. THE END! Lots of lists in history. I like lists a lot.

But French is messy and messy to me is like spiders to an arachnophobe. And Miss Belcher is - was, my French teacher. Not that she was from France. She was from Glasgow which is 896.21 kilometres from Paris. I know. I checked.

Anyway, I had French yesterday, my sixth class of the day, and she - Miss - was not in a very good mood. Isabella told me, so I knew. Isabella's smart, but in a different way to me, so she can always tell. I never can.

It was 2.15 on a Tuesday afternoon and this is what happened...

'Today we will work on verbs,' Miss Belcher barks, marching in. Everybody sits, stool legs scraping on the vinyl floor. Everybody but me.

'Kitty Maddocks, is that gum in your mouth? It is! Then swallow it, child. Anthony, sit up properly. PROPERLY!' She sniffs. She sniffs a lot. She's an habitual sniffer. Her eyes fall on me and she sighs. Then, in the French way, shortening the 'i', she says, 'Simon. Sit!'

Amid the sniggers and elbow nudging of the other kids, my bottom finds the top of the stool. But it is important she tells me or how will I know?

'Now! Pens down and TRY to copy my accent.

After me. Chanter.'

'Chanter,' the class mutters back.

'No, no, NO!' She thumps her desk on the last climactic 'NO'. 'With gusto, children. GUSTO! Now. Chanter.'

'CHANTER!' her students bellow.

Sullenly, I watch her. Not all of her, just her eyebrows. They always wriggle so and remind me of two furry caterpillars fighting on her brow. My eyes drift lower. She is very big-bosomed and very, very big-bottomed, and sort of reminds me of a bottle of Coca-Cola. A short bottle. I want to tell you how short but my ruler is only thirty centimetres long.

My gaze wanders to my desk and my...

Where IS my ruler?

'Simon!'

'SIMON!' the class howls back in unruly delight.

'No, no. Simon! Zip up your bag and put it on the floor.'

'I can't find my ruler,' I tell her. It is new; a birthday present from my dad. A Star Wars ruler with a Darth Vader sticker on it. I much prefer Star Trek to Star Wars but Dad will be upset if I can't find it.

Miss Belcher tuts and screws up her lips in such a way they remind me of a cat's bottom. 'You don't need your ruler. This is French, silly boy, not maths.'

'I wish it was maths,' I mutter into the murky depths of my satchel.

'Simon!' Blowing up like a bullfrog, she stomps over to me. 'Put your bag by your feet NOW! Or I will send you to Mr Cornfoot's room.'

Mr Cornfoot is the school janitor and his room is in the spidery cellar. Between 1751 and 1863, the school was a prison and they say murderers were kept down there.

But I just nod indifferently and glower at my desk. On it is my ink pen and two centimetres to the left of my ink pen is my Starship Enterprise NCC-1701-shaped rubber. But two centimetres to the left of my rubber there is a

big

scary

NOTHINGNESS

And it's not in my bag. 'It's not in my bag,' I tell her.

The class starts to giggle and Kitty Maddocks, the girl who swallowed the gum, starts to wheeze.

I feel so cross, so - out of sorts. How can she be this stupid? Why can she not understand? I begin to rock on my stool, my eyelids fluttering. I can feel the anger welling up in me, flooding my belly like hot bubbling acid. 'I can't find my ruler.' I say it much louder now. 'And it's not in my bag.'

One desk over, Isabella whispers, 'Calm down.' And a girl at the front of the classroom bellows, 'Miss! I think Kitty's choking.'

With a python-like hiss, Miss Belcher turns her back on me. 'Stop being so silly, Bridget. And Kitty, stop coughing. It's annoying.' She sniffs, juts out her jaw and stomps back to her desk. 'Now, BEGIN! Chanter.'

'Chanter,' burble the class. A class full of expectant eyes.

'Manger.'

'Manger.'

'What you lost, Nutter?' I look over at Anthony, the school bully. He is grinning away like a stowaway cat on a fishing trawler.

'I can't find my ruler,' I tell him, 'and it's not in my...'

'SIMON!' Miss Belcher howls, no longer in the French way, but with a strong Scottish lilt.

'MISS! HURRY! Kitty's all purply - and her right eye's sort of - bulging out.'

'BRIDGET!' she yells, her cheeks now all blotchy and red.

Then I begin to yell too, and when I yell I find it very difficult to stop. I growl and snarl. I kick over my desk. I even thump the wall. The class is no longer giggling. They just sit and watch me explode, chins to chests. The best show in town. Isabella is trying to pacify me. 'You probably just dropped it,' she is saying. 'Help me to look.'

Then...

I do it.

It is 2.43 on a Tuesday afternoon.

'Go to hell,' I hiss. And I wish fervently for Miss Belcher to be hit by a bus.

At 5.39, that very day...

She is.

TODAY

Chapter 2

'OY! NUTTER!'

THE NEXT DAY, WHEN I STEP OFF THE SCHOOL bus, I do not know of Miss Belcher's tragic accident. Everybody is staring at me, even Mr Parrot, who is on bus duty. But, to be honest, this happens to me pretty much every day. I think it's because I look a lot like a scarecrow, my mop of curls in need of scissors and a comb or, as Granny Spittle insists, a lawnmower or a power-saw.

Over by the gym, a boy prods his buddy in the ribs and flutters a hand at me. I begin to feel like a horse in a paddock and I wonder if anybody will ask to see my teeth.

To escape the looks, I lumber over to the bicycle shed and begin to count the tennis balls on the corrugated steel roof. I count twenty-seven - and ¾; the ¾ badly chewed up by a dog.

Shortly after, a second school bus crawls up and promptly vomits children all over the curb. 'GO ON! IN YOU GO!' howls Mr Parrot, ushering them over to the gate. The boys swagger. The girls strut. Fingers swish over telephone keypads and nobody bothers to look up.

I Think I Murdered Miss

I spot there is a new boy. He is ghostly pale and wiry thin, his body lost in a well-starched coffee-brown shirt, his hands hidden by the cuffs. There is a sort of waxy, buffed-up sheen to his skin as if he'd slept under a dripping candle and he has the alert look of a tomcat who can smell a nest of baby mice. For a split second he looks my way and scowls, his eyelids twitching like a bull bothered by a fly. Then, abruptly, he turns his back on me and limps over to the recycling bins.

With a puckered brow, I eye the price label sticking up from the back of his collar and wonder what's up with his leg. Then I pull a rolled-up copy of the 'Devilishly Difficult Puzzle Book' from my back pocket. It is not so difficult; not devilishly so anyway, but my father insists on getting it for me along with 'Roy of the Rovers', a football comic I never open. He thinks I do, but I don't.

It is crazily hot, so I unbutton my cardigan, top to bottom, button by button, and sit on a graffiti-scrawled bench in the shadow of the bicycle shed. There I thumb through my puzzle book to page six. This is what I see:

HOW MANY WORDS CAN YOU FIND?

The letter 'P' must be in every word.

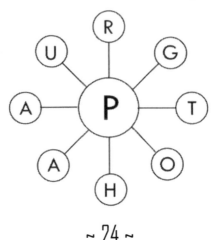

Simple. And, a second later, I scrawl twenty-two words under it.

Then I see this:

	+		−	x		÷		x		=	50

USING THE NUMBERS 1 TO 6,
FILL IN THE GAPS

This is child's play and, instantly, I scribble this:

$$2 + 4 - 1 \times 6 \div 3 \times 5 = 50$$

A little while later, Isabella discovers me there. But, by then, every puzzle in my book's been filled in and I'm back to counting tennis balls and listening to jazz on my iPod.

'Hi, Mop,' she calls, skipping over. She's so elegant and cool. I, on the other hand, am all elbowy and clumsy.

We only met in April when she and her family - mother, father, three brothers and a dog called Muffin - moved to the town. I helped her with her algebra homework; I still do and she, in turn, is sweet to me. She has freckly, apricot skin and gingery, corkscrew curls. It is summer now and she burns terribly.

'Don't stand in the sun,' I tell her sternly, switching off L Armstrong's husky tenor and standing up. 'You'll get cancer.'

'Hello Isabella,' she tweets. She's pretending to be me. 'How wonderful to see you.'

'It is?' she answers herself. 'Why Mop, how

sweet of you to say.'

Isabella thinks it is very important to swap dull chitchat in the mornings. My dad thinks so too. 'It is important to show interest in others,' he often tells me. So, with a sigh, I say, 'Hello Isabella.'

'Hello Mop.'

'How, er - wonderful to see you.'

'It is?' She grins and twists her nose. 'Why Mop, how sweet of you to say.'

I eye her distrustfully. She has a big, moon-shaped scar under her left eye so it looks as if her cheek is always smiling. It is very disconcerting. 'But no hugs,' I warn her, shuffling back.

Isabella lifts her eyes to the sky and stuffs her hands in her pockets. 'I will try to resist. It'll be difficult. I'm always drawn to boys with scarecrow curls and big, floppy cardigans, but I will do my very best.'

'Granny Spittle knitted me this,' I tell her snootily. I suddenly spy a button's dropped off, the third from the bottom, and now there's only a dangly bit of cotton.

'I know she did. Tell me, Mop, truthfully now, on a scale of 1 to 10, how blind is your granny?'

'She is not...' I stop. Isabella's trying to be funny; she's no fan of my woolly cardigan. I drop to my knees to hunt for the AWOL button.

'Get up,' mutters Isabella sternly. 'Everybody's looking.'

'I lost my button.' She's still in the sun and I begin to feel irritated. 'Cancer is not a joke,' I scold her.

She tuts and blows a raspberry at me. 'All right! Keep your shirt on. MUM!'

'I'm not your mum,' I inform her dryly, my cheek to the sizzling-hot cement, 'and shirts must be kept on, even in the summer. It's a school rule.'

With a roll of her eyes, her silver-buckled sandals (not school uniform; Mr Parrot will throw a hissy-fit if he sees them) shuffle her over to the shadow of the bicycle hut.

'Happy?'

'I'm not unhappy.' I find the button under the bench. Peeling chewing gum off it, I slip it in my pocket and clamber to my feet. Then, briskly, I inform her, 'My Gypsy Boy rose grew 0.27 of a centimetre in the last thirteen hours.'

'Wow! That's er, brill'. But listen to this...'

'Why is it brill'?' I interrupt her. 'It is just a fact; and why do you always shorten your words? Do you need to rush off to the loo or...?'

'Mop, this is important. Yesterday, Miss Belcher was hit by a bus. A Billy Smart's Circus bus. I saw it happen, after school just by the church. She was killed.'

She always calls me Mop. I think she thinks I'm scruffy. But combs do not interest me. Nor do barbers or gels.

'How odd,' I say thoughtfully. 'Only yesterday, I wished for her to be hit by a bus. But not a Billy Smart's Circus bus. Any bus, to be honest.'

'YOU DID!'

'Yes. The odds must be...' I frown and try to calculate them.

'Don't tell anybody.'

'I just told you.'

'Don't tell anybody, but me.'

The 'but' word! The horribly puzzling 'but' word. I try not to let it upset me. 'OK.' I nod. 'Why?'

'Why! WHY!' Her hands twirl like dizzy birds. 'Yesterday, you yelled at her. A lot. You even thumped your desk and told her to go to hell.'

'I kicked my desk,' I tell her wryly. 'I thumped the wall.'

'Whatever. The problem is, everybody will now think you cursed her.'

'Oh!' I feel as if a blindfold's been ripped from my eyes. Now I know why Mr Parrot and the other kids were eyeballing me when I got off the bus.

'But what they don't know is that you

ACTUALLY DID!' Her eyes dart to the recycling bins and the new boy who is sitting just by them. A shadow seems to envelop her lips, darkening her words. 'They'll call you a witch,' she whispers.

'A wizard,' I correct her. 'I'm a boy.'

'That's not funny.'

'I was being funny?'

She blows out her cheeks in a way I just don't get. I often see dad do it and, on Saturday, Mrs Radinski in the Spar did it when I asked her, for the two hundred and sixth time, or was it the two hundred and seventh, if she planned to sell Star Trek comics in her shop. In fact, pretty much everybody I meet seems to do it. It is, I think, a look invented just for me.

No, it WAS the two hundred and sixth. I

remember now. She'd told me not to bother her at the end of a very long day. It had been 8.30 in the morning.

'By the way, Kitty's off today,' Isabella says. 'But don't worry, I think she's OK. Bridget told me in netball.'

Now I'm totally and utterly flummoxed. I know who Kitty is. I know she almost choked in French class. But what I don't know, what I cannot understand, is why Isabella is telling me this; and why she thinks I'm worrying about it.

I ask her.

Isabella sighs (I have problems with sighs too) and returns to her 'cheek blowing'.

'OY! NUTTER!' I turn to see Anthony, my only enemy, clumping over to me. I say 'only enemy', but there is another. The evil Klingon Empire, the enemy of everybody in the Galaxy.

Anthony's torso is big, his shoulders bigger and his skull is topped with black steely wool just like a Brillo pad. He smells of battered cod too; his mum owns the Frying Nemo, the chip shop in town, and there's a splodge of jam on his shirt. Strawberry, I think.

He stops just short of me, his banana-fingered hands on his hips.

'Just let him be,' Isabella says to him. 'You know how upset he gets.'

'Oh, I know. Everybody knows. Everybody in French anyway.' He titters hollowly and pulls a wooden ruler from his pocket. 'Tell me, Nutter, is this yours?'

I spot the Darth Vader sticker and nod. A crowd is now forming, the kids jostling for a better look. Even the new boy is there, no doubt keen to fit in and look cool. The school bell rings and I wonder with a nervy swallow where Mr Parrot is.

Anthony holds the ruler out to me and I go to grab it. But, then, with a snort, he snaps it in two.

My lips suddenly feel all dry and swollen and I begin to play with the strap on my satchel. Isabella, who knows me all too well, whispers, 'Don't tell him any flower facts.'

'A fossilised rose over 35,000,000 years old was discovered in the US,' I promptly tell him.

Next to me, Isabella sighs - I don't know why - and the mob of kids begin to chuckle excitedly.

'But the oldest living rose is in Germany. It is over 1,000 years old and grows on a wall.'

'DORK!' yells a boy in the crowd, his anonymous foot finding my right bottom cheek.

'GEEK!' hollers another.

'The circus is in town,' Anthony says, a glint in his eye. 'And I bet they need a new act. You know the sort of thing. ROLE UP! ROLE UP! See the Volcano Boy blow his top.'

I can tell he's insulting me, so why, I wonder, is he smiling. My dad, Isabella too, they smile when they try to help me. Is he trying to help me then? Perhaps he thinks I want a job in the circus. Perhaps he wants a job too. Then, I will try to assist him. It is important to lend a hand. Dad told me.

'I don't want to work in the circus,' I say matter-of-factly. 'But if you do, I will try to help. Now, let me see, acrobats tend to be thin so probably not the best job for you. There's juggling. Stilts. Lion taming.' I frown, lost in thought. Then I snap my fingers. 'I know! A clown's chubby, and you don't need to be good at anything. You just need to be stupid. Perfect! You can be a clown.'

Anthony's top lip flips up in a snarl and he thumps his fist in his hand. 'You cheeky little...'

'Go away,' yells Isabella, trying to squeeze between us.

But he elbows her in the ribs, knocking her to her knees.

I want to help her up - I so want to - but the thought of laying my hand on her, on anybody, fills me with horror. I watch her clamber to her feet. Then, with fury simmering under my skin, I turn on the bully.

'Don't let him upset you,' Isabella whispers to me, brushing dust off her skirt. 'That's what he wants.' She nods to the mob of heckling kids. 'What they all want.'

But today I do not go crazy, I do not blow my top. I'm a pot of bubbling water and I was just lifted off the hob. I simply say, 'I hope you get hit by a bus too.'

Anthony gawps at me and a hush falls on the crowd. It's as if I just told a joke but it turned out not to be very funny. Even Isabella seems speechless. 'What did you just say?' the bully growls.

I feel my newly-discovered bravery start to ebb, but I clench my jaws - and my bottom - and with only a tiny tremor, I say softly, 'Miss Belcher upset me and look what happened to her.'

With a wolfish snarl, the boy steps up to me, his fists up. I cower away but he just drops the broken shards of ruler by my feet. 'Y' a nutter and a loser,' he spits, 'and I need a new punch bag.'

'OY! YOU LOT!' Mr Parrot at long last. 'The bell's rung. Off to class.'

For a second, Anthony just glowers at me, and even I can tell now is not the moment to bring up the splodge of jam on his shirt. Is it strawberry? Difficult to tell.

He barks a laugh and turns to go.

Then I say it. I just can't help myself. It's as if there's a playful devil sitting on my shoulder, egging me on. 'There's jam on your shirt.'

By my elbow, Isabella throws up her hands in

despair.

'I think it's strawberry. Is it?'

He stops and looks back at me, a sneer widening his nostrils. 'No,' he growls, pincering the blemished cotton between his thumb and fingers. 'This here is blood, and by tomorrow there'll be blood on yours too.'

I swallow and watch him swagger off through the crowd.

Chapter 3

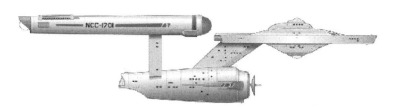

HOCUS POCUS!
YOUR CURLY WURLY'S A CROCUS

I LOVE THE SCHOOL LIBRARY. IT IS UP ON THE TOP floor, well away from stamping feet and playful yells. Every lunch, I go there. I collect my book 'Woodlands and the Flowers that Grow There' from the Nature shelf. It is always the seventh book in, wedged between 'A History of Moss' and a very dirty copy of 'Weeds Need Love Too'. I call it 'my' book because, oddly, nobody seems interested in it but me. Then I slump down in a dusty corner to read.

The library is my secret spot. My cave. Anthony's not much of a bookworm so he never sets foot in here. So I feel safe. Almost comfortable. Here, it is OK to sit by myself. I look, I think, much less pitiful. Just another person who wants to be on his own and enjoy a good story. I feel less 'different' here, less of a 'nutter'.

Munching on the ham and pickle roll my dad packed for me, I study a drawing of a daffodil. The cup, I spot, is too big and the petals too small. I will write to the author, a Dr Jemima Brooks, and let her know. It will be my three hundred and fifty-sixth letter to her with no reply. I often wonder why...

Hurrying feet interrupt my thoughts and I look up to see Isabella winding her way between a six foot paper-mache model of Roald Dahl's BFG and the World War Two shelf. She pulls up a stool and parks her bottom on it.

'What do we do if Anthony gets hit by a bus too?' she blankly asks me.

'He won't be,' I answer, burying my curly locks still further into my book.

'But what if he is?'

'If he is, he is. Accidents happen and that's all it will be.' Slowly, I say, 'I'm not a wizard, Isabella.' I always call her Isabella. I never shorten it to Izzy or Bella. Always Isabella. 'I'm not Harry Potter,' I add.

I can feel her eyeing the top of my skull. Then,

slowly, stressing every word, she says, 'Try and do a spell.'

Slowly, I lower my book. 'Sorry, what?'

Ignoring me, she digs her hand in her school bag and plucks out a droopy-looking Curly Wurly. 'Turn this into a flower.'

I look at her blankly.

'Turn this Curly Wurly,' she unwraps the top half and flaps it vigorously in my face, 'into a flower.'

'How?'

She lifts her shoulders. 'I don't know, do I? I'm not the wizard.'

'Nor am I,' I tell her starchly.

'OK! OK! Don't get your knickers in a twist.'

'I'm not...'

'I know! I know! It's just a saying. Honestly,

Mop, you can be so annoying.'

Biting off a chunk of Curly Wurly, she shuts her eyes and begins to hum softly.

'Y-fronts,' I mutter.

'Shut up! I'm trying to think.' She starts to rock on her stool and seems to be in deep thought.

After a few seconds, I ask her, a little incredulously, 'Is this how you think?'

She nods, her eyes still shut and chews off a second chunk.

I snort. 'No wonder you only ever get 'C's.'

'I've got it!' she howls.

'Shush,' I hiss. 'This is the library.'

'Try a rhyme. Try er, Hocus Pocus! Your Curly Wurly's a, er...'

'Crocus?'

'Yes. YES! Very good. A crocus.' She hands me the toffee bar. 'Go on. Try it.'

'There's not much left to try it on,' I observe.

I wither under her frosty stare. 'Just do it, Mop.'

'OK, Bossy Boots.' Anything if it will put to rest this crazy, 'over the top' fantasy of hers and I can return to the tranquil world of woodland flowers. I lift up the Curly Wurly...

'Stop!'

'I didn't start,' I tell her dryly.

'You need a wand.'

'A wand?'

'Yes.' She nods enthusiastically. 'Everybody knows, to do a magic spell you need a magic wand.'

'Everybody!' I look at her in astonishment.

'You think everybody knows that!?' I'm beginning to wonder if she's not totally off her rocker. 'I know this will be a terrible shock to you, but there's no wand in my pocket. Or in my bag. Not even a floppy toy shop wand with a bunch of flowers hidden in it.'

Unperturbed, she hands me a stubby pencil. 'Try this. And wave it around a bit.'

'Isabella, this is ridiculous.' I study the pencil. 'And this needs sharpening.'

'If you do it and the Curly Wurly's still a Curly Wurly, I'll stop...'

'Annoying me?'

'Yes.'

'Honestly?'

'Yes.'

Reluctantly, I nod. 'Fine,' I growl, lifting up the

pencil. At once, Isabella begins to shuffle back on her stool.

'It's not going to blow up, you know,' I admonish her.

'No, I don't know. That's why I'm moving back.'

I chew briskly on my lower lip. There is, annoyingly, a tiny, tiny element of logic to her words.

'Hocus Pocus,' I begin.

'No, no, no,' she barks, reminding me for a moment of the bus-pulped Miss Belcher. 'Chant it.'

'Chant it.' I sigh. 'OK.' So, bobbing the pencil (wand) up and down, I chant, 'Hocus Pocus! Your Curly Wurly's a crocus.'

Isabella looks expectantly at the toffee bar but there's no puff of smoke and absolutely no sign of any petal growth.

Shuffling back up to me, I watch her put the Curly Wurly to her nostrils. 'It smells a little flowery,' she says thoughtfully.

'Oh, stop being so stupid.' I hand her back the pencil and, thankfully, peer down at my book. 'Did you know there's a flower that smells of rotting flesh?'

'No, and to be perfectly honest I didn't want to. Mop, this is too important.'

'But you just swore to me if the Curly Wurly didn't...'

'My fingers were crossed. Mop, after school we must find a way to stop Anthony from being run over by a bus.'

I look to her in horror, my lips forming a perfect 'O'. 'But today's Wednesday,' I whine.

'There's Chess Club after school. I never miss Chess Club. Ever. Then Star Trek's on. I never miss Star Trek. Ever. And Dad cooks spaghetti on Wednesday.'

'I never miss spaghetti,' she mimics me. 'Ever.'

'Well, I never do,' I mumble.

She rolls her eyes. 'Yesterday, you were so angry with Miss Belcher, you kicked over your stool...'

'No, I kicked over my...'

'Whatever! You were angry with her and told her to go to hell and later that day she did. Then you told Anthony in front of almost every kid in school you hoped he'd be hit by a bus too. Well, let's just say he IS. Everybody will think you cursed him - and her. They'll call you a witch.'

'Wizard,' I correct her. My belly suddenly feels awfully hollow. I remedy the problem by snatching back the Curly Wurly.

'They'll burn you,' says Isabella, darkly.

'There's been no witch burning in this country for over two hundred years,' I coldly tell her. 'Two hundred and two to be correct - and three months.'

Isabella looks at me in astonishment. 'How can you possibly know that?'

'Mr Parrot told us two weeks ago in History.' Now it is my turn to roll my eyes. 'You were there, remember? Everybody knows.'

'I think you'll find everybody KNEW two weeks ago, for perhaps ten seconds, just after Mr Parrot told them. Then they promptly forgot.' Her eyes narrow. 'I bet you even remember her name.'

'No,' I say defensively.

'Oh. Pity. I soooo wanted to know...'

'Barbara Zdunk in 1811.'

'AH HA! You do remember. Honestly, Mop, you need a hobby. And, no, watching Star Trek is not a hobby.'

I open my Curly Wurly-filled mouth to protest.

'And nor is nerdy chess or gobbling spaghetti,' she adds with a grin.

I grunt and, grumpily, flip over the page in my book.

'Mop, I know this is difficult for you,' she pulls her stool up even closer, pinching back the Curly Wurly - hippos feed less, 'but...'

'Stop saying the word 'but'.' I flap a hand at her. 'And I need my space.'

'Oh, sorry. The two-foot rule. I forgot.'

I stare daggers at her till she drags her stool away.

'You know, I wasn't planning to hug you,' she utters snootily.

'Good. I'm not much of a hugger.'

Her lips quirk up. 'Yes, I know. You tell me every day. You tell everybody every day. Mop, listen to me, if anything, ANYTHING happens to Anthony now, they will blame you. Everybody will think you're a devil-kid. You'll probably be carted off to a loony asylum. Doctors will prod you and hook your eyeballs up to a car battery.'

'But Chess Club...'

'Mop!'

'And Star Trek.'

Suddenly, her eyes light up and she springs to

her feet. 'I know, why don't we find a map of the town?'

Gloomily, I nod. She knows how much I love maps. Chuntering about how much I enjoy my dad's spaghetti too, I follow Isabella's flapping heels over to the library computer. She sits and, over her shoulder, I watch her bring up Google Maps and type in 'Trotswood', the name of our town. Instantly, a street map pops up: shops, pubs, bus stops and all.

Chewing thoughtfully on the end of her blunt pencil, Isabella scowls at the screen. Oddly, it looks as if the tip of the pencil is glowing pink. I frown and rub my eyes. My mind must be playing tricks on me.

'At the end of school,' she says, hastily dropping the pencil in her bag, 'when Anthony walks home, we must find a way to stop him going by any bus stops.'

'Why?'

'Why! WHY! Then there's less risk of him being run over, you plonker.'

My jaw clunks, yes, CLUNKS to my chest, and my eyes truly spin. Yes. YES! I can feel them - SPINNING! I suddenly feel all hot and clammy and I pull off my cardigan. 'But, but...'

'I thought you didn't like the word 'but'.'

'THAT'S CRAZY!' All I want to do is enjoy 'Woodlands and the Flowers that Grow There' and my ham and pickle roll.

'No, Mop, it's not.' She glowers at the screen. 'Anthony and his mum, they live over the chip shop, yes?'

'Yes,' I utter glumly.

'Oh! But look. There must be hundreds of bus stops between the school and there.' She looks up at me, her eyes all big and innocent. 'But there must be a different way. I just wish I was a bit cleverer. Like you.'

I know she's manipulating me, but a test's a test and I'm good at tests.

I study the map for a moment, the cogs in my skull twirling, then, 'There is a different way,' I say reluctantly. 'If he walks up Gunpowder Street, not Candy Lane, then right over Shoots Bridge, by the Spar, that's where they don't sell Star Trek comics, and Big Baps Café, then he will not go by any bus stops at all.'

Isabella looks at the screen and then back at me, her eyes narrow and thoughtful. 'I think you're right.'

'I know I'm right,' I say indignantly. 'My IQ is over a hundred and fifty.'

'Is that good?'

'No. A hundred's good.'

She props a thin smile on her lips. 'Then that is the way he must go.'

'But there's no way he will,' I protest.

'There's that 'but' word.'

I ignore her and jab the screen. 'Look, when he walks out of the school, he'll turn left. It's only 1.5kms that way. He'll go up Candy Lane, by the tennis ball factory and six, no, seven bus stops. If he walks say, 6kms per hour, he will be home in fifteen minutes.'

Isabella winks at me in what I think must be a 'conspiring' way. Then she says, 'Not if he's chasing you.'

Chapter 4

GREEN FOOD, PARROTS AND PAPER CUPS

ROOSTING ON THE LOWEST BRANCH OF A chestnut tree, I turn to Isabella and say, 'I detest green food, parrots and paper cups. Mostly paper cups.'

I watch her eyebrows knit together. 'Paper cups. Why paper cups?'

'Well, they go so soft and mushy, don't they? When they get wet.' I swell up my chest. 'A cup's job,' I lecture her, 'is to hold a drink, be it orange, lemon, water - sparkling or still - apple, cherry, kiwi...'

'Do you plan to list all of them?'

'No. Why? Do you want me to?'

'No, not really.'

'But a paper cup,' I carry on, 'when it is all soft and soggy, won't hold orange, lemon, water...'

'Sparkling or still,' murmurs Isabella.

'...apple, cherry, kiwi or even,' I eye her expectantly, 'python's milk.'

With hooded lids, she swivels on her bottom to look at me. 'OK, I know you're dying to tell me, so let's get it over with. Who drinks python's milk?'

'In the Congo; that's in Africa...'

'I know where it is, Smarty Pants. I'm not a

toddler.'

'Oh! Good. Well, anyway, in the Congo; that's in...'

'Mop!'

'Africa,' I murmur, 'they drink it to ward off evil spirits.'

'Wow! What a lot of er, interesting stuff you know.'

I eye her keenly. Is she being sarcastic, I wonder. Mocking me? No, probably not. I think she's just impressed by my worldly intellect. So I say, 'Yes. Yes, I do.'

Rummaging in her bag, Isabella pulls out a gigantic Twix. She's such a choc monster. Odd, she's so slim.

'So in the Congo they drink python's milk from paper cups?'

'No! Stupid. Paper cups don't work. Were you not,' I sigh, 'oh, forget it.'

She sighs too and I frown. I only understand my sighs. Never hers.

We sit for a moment, legs dangling from the tree branch, Isabella chomping on her foot-long toffee fingers. It is, I think, a very 'correct' sort of tree; tall and bushy and full of spiky, green-shelled conkers. It is so bushy, nobody can see us up here, and it is only twenty feet from the school doors. The perfect spot to ambush Anthony from.

'Go on then, spill it,' says Isabella, spitting crumbs, 'what's your problem with parrots?'

'When I was six, I went in a pet shop with my mum, and this cockatoo asked me for a bag of nuts.'

'So?'

'So I didn't have a bag of nuts, did I. It upset me terribly.'

She grins and looks up at the sky. 'Yes, well, forgetting your nuts can be very upsetting.'

I grin too, showing her all of my teeth like a wildly overjoyed tiger.

'Your smile is very, er - powerful,' she says wryly. 'You turn it on: lots of teeth and gums, or you turn it off: stroppy old git. There's no sly lift of the lips. No - dripping tap. Sort of scary, you know.'

I nod, gravely. But, to be honest, I'm stumped. Her words - all mumbo jumbo gibberish to me.

'What upsets you the most?' I ask her. I do not want to know, but it is good manners to ask. My dad told me.

'Most?' She drums her fingers on her chin. 'Er, you.'

She is chuckling as she talks so I'm confident she's joking.

'Just joking.'

I thought so and I try to copy her toffee-blotted smile. I smile a lot in the mirror so I know how to.

I find it very difficult to know when to smile and when not to. So my rule is, if everybody - anybody is smiling, I smile too. As big as I possibly can. It seems to work. Mostly. Except when I'm watching Star Trek II, The Wrath of Khan and Khan is smiling evilly. Smiling. EVILLY! That's just crazy.

'Smelly boys upset me,' Isabella suddenly says, 'and broken lamps. Oh, and dog poo,' she adds with a snap of her fingers. 'Not all dog poo. Just the poo I step in.'

There is, I think, no reply to this, so I do not even try. I simply nod and, slyly, try to sniff my right armpit.

School is over for the day and almost everybody has left. Even Mr Cornfoot, the janitor, pedalling away on his old rusty bicycle. But Anthony's got Boxing Club and that ends at 4 o'clock. I study my 50th Anniversary Star Trek watch. The shorter 'Spock' hand is almost to the four, the longer 'Kirk' hand creeping up on the twelve. Only thirty seconds till crunch time.

'But what if he corners me?' I snivel. 'He's the School Boxing Champ.'

'No, he's not.'

'He's not? Honestly? Well, that's good news.'

'He's the North of England School Boxing Champ.'

I swallow.

'It was in all the newspapers. Anthony knocked the other boy out.'

'This is not helping,' I tell her.

'His opponent - I can't remember his name,' she titters, 'a little ironic, he also can't remember it. But the doctors think he'll recover. Probably. In a month or two.'

My shoulders sink. Anthony will murder me.

'Chin up, Mop. Then he can hit it harder. HA! HA! Get it?'

I let out a low whimpering snivel.

'Sorry. Just joking. Anyway, I bet you're the best player in the Chess Club.'

Frowning, I look up. 'Yes, I am,' I say slowly. I

often find it difficult to follow Isabella's logic. 'But my skill in chess will not stop Anthony's fists.'

'Why not pin him down with your rook...'

I blow out my cheeks. Now I get it. Isabella's trying to be funny.

'...or boot him in the ribs with your horse?'

'It is not a horse,' I tell her haughtily. 'It is a knight.'

I only wish I could call up my knight. Then, with the help of my two intrepid bishops, block him in a corner, my queen swooping in to deliver the knock-out blow...

'Keep your eyes peeled,' murmurs Isabella, crumpling up the Twix wrapper and stuffing it in her pocket. 'He'll be here soon.'

I nod and, rapturously, we gaze at the school

door. But I'm dying to know and I can't hold it in, so I whisper, 'Why 'peeled'?'

'What?'

'You can peel a potato, a carrot, a banana, a...

'I'll pay you to stop.'

'How much?'

'MOP!'

'I'm just saying, you can't peel your eyeballs. Well, you can, but it'll hurt a lot and it won't help you to see any better.'

I feel Isabella's elbow in my ribs and I draw back. 'I see him,' she says.

With a churning stomach, I peer down and I soon spot Anthony lolloping down the school steps. I see he is still in his sports kit: navy shorts and a wrinkly, sweat-stained t-shirt, 'BORN TO BE BAD' in fat, crimson letters on the chest. Oddly, he's put his boots back on, his plimsolls scrunched up like tissue paper in his left fist. I wonder what they did to upset him.

'Now what?' I whisper. I do, in fact, know the plan, but now Isabella's seen the t-shirt and what happened to the poor plimsolls, I'm cheerfully optimistic she must be thinking what I'm thinking: let's just sit here till he's left and then scurry off home to watch TV.

'Now, you run,' she says.

I nod despondently and check my watch. Star Trek begins in less than two hours. If I'm lucky, Anthony will be hungry for his dinner and will only batter me for a minute or two. Then I will still see the end.

'And remember,' she grips the sleeve of my cardigan, 'he must follow you, so try and annoy him.'

'Annoy him. How?'

'Don't worry, Mop, everybody finds you annoying. Just be yourself.' She lifts her eyebrow expectantly so I nod. Then, with a toothy grin and with no warning whatsoever, she elbows me off the branch.

I land on the hot tarmac with a bone-crunching thud, only a foot or so in front of Anthony's scuffed boots. Clambering shakily to my feet, I glance back up at the branch but Isabella is nowhere to be seen. I scowl. How did she...

'Well, well,' he shoots me such a wintry leer, I actually feel cold, 'it seems a nut's dropped off the tree. Rotten, I bet.' With a snigger, Anthony steps up to me.

I look up at the school bully. He is so much taller than me; wider too. It's almost as if I'm at the zoo and suddenly I find myself in the cage with the gorilla. With a nervy swallow, I sputter, 'C-conkers drop in September and October, not July. Idiot.'

His jaw hardens and, if the plimsolls in his balled-up fist were capable of it, they'd now be howling and begging for mercy. Isabella, it seems, was spot on: I AM very annoying. With a whimper, I twist on my heels and scarper.

I sprint down Gunpowder Street, by ASDA and then left by the Nobody Inn, a pub with a Wellington boot-shaped knocker on the door. I look over my shoulder and spot Anthony just turning the corner. He is smiling. Smiling! Just like the evil Khan in Star Trek when he's trying to kill Kirk.

Oddly, my hunter is only jogging and seems to be in no hurry to catch me. He must be enjoying the hunt too much.

I remember the words of Khan in the film: 'I'll chase him round the moons of Nibia, and round Antare's Maelstrom, and round Perdition's flame before I give him up.' I clench my teeth and try to speed up a bit.

The problem is, I'm not a very fast runner. In fact, to be perfectly honest, I'm by far the slowest in school. Slower than Polly Smith and she's fatter than a milking cow. Slower even than Alfo, her older brother, and he's got the most terrible limp. It says on the wall, in the boys' loos, Polly tripped over and flattened her brother's foot. Poor kid.

You see, I have the worst handicap of all. I must jump over all the cracks in the street. I never ever step on cracks. EVER! If I do, my world will end. If I do, googly-eyed monsters will creep out from under my bed and rip off my limbs.

So, when I run, I sort of hop from paving slab to paving slab in a sort of zig-zaggy, wobbly-kangaroo sort of way.

Wiping salty water from my eyes, I finally spot Shoots Bridge. It is very old and very narrow and spans the town's river. If I can make it over the river and by Big Baps Café, I will be on the High Street. It will be crowded with shoppers and Anthony will not dare to attack me there.

I get to the bridge and run up and over it, my boots clumping a drum rhythm on the wooden timbers.

By the Post Office, I try to turn the corner, but there, directly in my way, is a child's tricycle. I attempt to hurdle it but my boot thumps the bell and with a 'Ding!', I cartwheel to the path.

With my knee feeling as if it's on fire, I clamber awkwardly to my feet. Everything seems to hurt: my leg, my elbow, the little finger on my left hand; I even stubbed my big toe. And, to top it all off, it looks as if I lost another button off my cardigan.

'Oy! Nutter!' A yell from behind. 'When I catch you, I'm going to batter you to a bloody pulp.'

In terror, I look back. Yes, there he is, just by the bridge. Even from here I can see he looks very, VERY angry. It's the way he's snarling and spitting and clenching his fists. Oh, and the 'bloody pulp' comment. In spite of the sun, a cold shiver runs down my spine. It seems he is no longer enjoying the hunt.

Why am I even doing this, I wonder crossly. There's just no way Anthony's going to be hit by a bus too. What happened to Miss Belcher was just an accident; bad luck, for her and for me. I blame Isabella. If I don't put a stop to this crazy fantasy of hers I will end up in hospital. In splints. ON A DRIP!

I turn to run on but I spot a man on the street in a yellow vest. He is resting his elbows on a jackhammer and drinking from a paper cup. But it is not the paper cup that upsets me the most - although it is very upsetting. To my horror, the cement by his feet is a puzzle of cracks; and there's no way by them all. But I can't stand on a crack. I just can't...

What feels very much like a ten-ton truck whollops me in the back and I topple over, smacking my upper lip on the path. With blood flooding my mouth, I twist slowly over and look up to find Anthony towering over me. Pins of terror prickle my scalp. Even I cannot mistake the look of glee in his pot lid eyes.

Like a fat boy on a muffin, he is on me, booting me in the ribs and rolling me over and over on the hard pavement. I cry out in agony. 'Stop,' I whimper.

He checks his watch and tuts. 'Y' lucky I'm in a rush, Nutter, or I'd kick all the stuffin' out of you. But I just remembered I'm off to the circus at five, so this,' he boots me in the leg, 'must do the job.' Gripping his plimsolls by the lace, he droops them over his shoulder and turns to go.

But not the way I want him to.

NO!' I cry. I must be crazy. 'Don't go that way. Go past Big Babs Café. It's much shorter.'

He stops and slowly turns to look at me. Even I can see the distrust in the arch of his eyebrows. He's wondering why I'm helping him. Not surprising, he did just clobber me.

'I'm different,' I tell him, in a poor attempt at justifying my words.

He scowls. 'What?'

I mentally scratch my brow. How can I get this dimwit to understand my problem? 'Stuff upsets me,' I finally say, 'and it will upset me if you go the wrong way.'

For just over a second, he wavers. The

opportunity to upset me must be very tempting. But, thankfully, he's in a hurry and the thought of missing the circus wins the day. 'Nutter,' he mutters and, with a shrug, he stomps off.

I watch him go. Then slowly I sit up. I did it. I actually did it. There are no bus stops that way so there's hardly any risk of Anthony being hit by a bus. Now nobody will think I'm a devil-kid, I won't be carted off to a loony asylum, and doctors will not prod me and hook my eyeballs up to a car battery.

Exactly three seconds later, a distressed-looking Isabella runs over and helps me to my feet.

'I'm OK,' I tell her curtly, levering her well-meaning fingers off my caridgan shirt sleeve. 'I don't like being...'

'Yes, yes, I know. The two-foot rule.' Sighing, she pulls a hanky from her pocket and hands it to me. 'I'm just trying to help.'

'Help. HELP! Just look at me. I look as if, as if...'

'You were run over by a bus?'

'Exactly. This is what happens when I let you help me.'

Isabella says nothing but simply looks on as I dab my bloody lip.

'It feels swollen,' I whimper, prodding it with the tip of my tongue.

'It is. Very. Oh, and you lost another button off your floppy cardigan.'

'I know,' I snap. 'I know.'

'Such a pity. And it's so fluffy and lumpy - flumpy. Ooh! I invented a new word. Oh well, now you'll have to dump it.'

I glare daggers at her. 'I'm not dump...' Suddenly, I remember her vanishing act in the Chestnut tree. 'Where did you go?'

'When?'

'When you brutally chucked me out of the tree. I looked for you but...'

'I was there on the branch.'

'No, I looked.'

'You probably just missed me.' She grins. 'I'm very slim.'

'Isabella, the branch was brown and your skirt is purple.'

'Maybe you thought I was a plum.'

'It was a Chestnut tree. It was full of conkers.'

'Oh! Well, anyway,' her hands find her hips, 'did Anthony just tell you he's off to the circus tonight?'

My hands find my hips too. 'And how do you know that?'

'I'm a plum.' She looks me directly in the eyes. 'Plums know stuff.'

I sniff scornfully, willing my eyes to out burn hers. The girl's bonkers. 'Yes, he is. With any luck, the stinker will get gobbled up by a...'

'MOP! NO! Don't say it. It might happen.'

'Oh, yes,' I return to dabbing my lip. 'Better not risk it.'

'No,' Isabella agrees, nodding vigorously. 'Better not.'

I drop my gaze to my boots, spot my fugitive button and pick it up. 'OK, so, I'm off home to...'

'Mop, you can't just go. The bus that hit Miss Belcher will be at that circus. What if...'

I Think I Murdered Miss

'NO!' I storm, my temper rising with my eyes. I feel horribly, terribly uncomfortable; a fish out of water. I need order. I need Star Trek, episode twenty-five, when a monster attacks Spock. I need...

MY DAD'S SPAGHETTI!

'I did my bit,' I tell her. 'I stopped him walking by any bus stops and to thank me, he split my lip. If you want to play hero, play hero, but I'm off home to enjoy spaghetti and the END of Star Trek.'

I sniff and toss her hanky back to her. Then, with considerable difficulty, I slowly turn and limp off.

'Well, you walk like a robot,' she yells after me.

'No, I don't,' I yell back.

'Yes, you do.'

Chapter 5

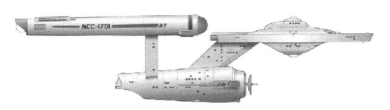

DROWNING FISH

WHEN I FINALLY HOBBLE IN THE FRONT DOOR, MY dad almost keels over when he sees all the cuts to my cheeks, elbows and lips and he instantly sets about me with swabs, scissors and safety pins. Then he puts me in the kitchen, in front of a fork and a bowl of piping-hot spaghetti.

Cup in hand, Dad pulls up a stool and sits too. 'It must hurt terribly,' he says.

'Yes.' I reply, shovelling a forkful of spaghetti in my mouth. I chew it in my left cheek well away from my swollen right.

'And this kid's bicycle...'

'Tricycle,' I correct him.

'Tricycle, then. You say it was just left there in the street?'

'Yes.'

'And you tripped over it?'

'Yes.'

Dad sips his coffee and sighs. I think he finds me difficult.

He's sort of chubby, my dad, and the crown of his skull is shiny and bald. He often tells me, jokingly (I think), 'If I draw a big H on it, helicopters will try to land there.' He works a lot with wood. It says 'Odd Job Man' on the poster he put up in the Spar, but he's not just that. He's amazing with hammers, screwdrivers and chisels. He can knock up a French dresser from broken wood tossed in a skip and he can chisel anything from anything. My dad's not just an odd job man, he's an artist.

'Did you say you were running?'

'Jogging.'

'But you never run. Or jog.'

'Spaghetti night,' I explain. 'I didn't want to miss it.'

'I see. And you fell on what? A landmine?'

'There's no...' I stop. 'A joke, yes?'

'Yes, Simon. A joke.'

Quickly, I wolf down my spaghetti, resting the dirty fork in the bowl, perfectly parallel to the edge of the table.

'Two buttons dropped off my cardigan,' I tell him. 'Will you sew them back on for me?'

Dad drums his fingertips on the table top and slowly nods. I think he suspects I'm not telling him the truth.

'When?' I quiz him.

'Tomorrow.'

'When tomorrow?'

'When I get up.'

'At 7.47 then.'

'Yes. At 7.47.'

I nod contentedly. 'I will go up to my room now. Star Trek's on.'

'OK, son.'

Slipping off my stool, I limp old-mannishly over to the door.

'Simon!' Reluctantly, I stop and look back at him. 'Here's your new Devilishly Difficult Puzzle Book. It's the July issue. I picked it up yesterday from the Spar.'

I lumber back over and he hands it to me.

'Oh, and I put Roy of the Rovers on the end of your bed.' With a grin, he adds, 'You can put it in your bottom drawer with the rest of them.'

'I will,' I say.

'You know, if there's a problem at school, if anybody's bullying you...'

'No, there's not.' I shift awkwardly from foot to foot. If only I was Kirk. Then I'd contact Scotty in Engineering and order him to beam me directly to my bedroom.

'Dad, do I walk like a robot?' I suddenly ask him.

'Em,' he rubs his chin, 'a little bit. But a super-cool robot with, er - sensors and a big battery.'

'A dilithium battery?'

'Yep.'

I nod. 'That's OK then.'

Dad gets to your feet and I can tell he wants to try and hug me. 'I'm not much of a hugger,' I remind him sternly.

'Yes, I know.' A tiny smile plays on his lips. 'But did YOU know tonight's Star Trek will be on for six hours, episode eighteen to twenty-three, back to back.'

'No,' I cry. 'Wonderful!' Then I frown thoughtfully. 'Eighteen is the episode with the...'

'Gorn, yes.'

'He's so cool.'

Dad nods. 'Yes, he is. Off you trot then.'

For the shortest of seconds, I rest my hand on his arm. It is the very best I can do. 'A horse trots,' I tell him. Then I turn and limp from the kitchen.

My bedroom is very important to me. Like the school library, it is where I hide from the world. In it there is my bed, the corners tucked in, my cuddly toy hen perched on the evenly fluffed-up pillows, and, next to it, on the window sill, sits my Gypsy Boy rose and a silver-framed photo of my mum. Star Trek posters cover almost every foot of the walls, but for my TV, a mirror and a tiny poster of Trotswood FC I put up in a corner to keep my dad happy. Over by the door there is a shelf and this is where I store my CDs; mostly old stuff, jazz, Louis Armstrong and Art Tatum. Next to the CDs, I keep my trumpet and my Star Trek comics, the comics all in date order, June 5, 1967 to September 25, 1998. And finally, at the very end, my Star Trek models: Kirk, Spock,

McCoy, Sulu and Uhura. I'm still looking for Scotty and Chekov. There is a chest of drawers in the corner full of shirts, socks, y-fronts and Star Trek uniforms, all ironed and folded. And, sitting on top of it, a 1/500 scale model of the Starship Enterprise NCC-1701.

After running a duster over the sleek, frisbee-shaped hull, I lumber over to my rose. Everybody always says how pretty a rose is and I want to know why. So I'm compiling data in a book. Then, when the flower is fully grown, I will draw graphs, lots of graphs, and from them I will work out why. It can't just be the velvety feel of the petals. It can't just be the smell.

It looks a little taller than it did yesterday so I hunt in my satchel for my ruler. Then I remember Anthony snapped it in two. 'DIMWIT!' I snarl, a rumble of thunder handily drowning out my vulgarity. The wall is very thin and I don't want to upset Mrs Cherry, the old spinster next door.

The sun in the window dims - I suspect the thunder cloud - so I plod over to my desk and switch on the lamp.

Looking at myself in the wall mirror, I decide I look terrible. My blond curls don't just sit on my skull, they explode off it, and my Adam's apple is much too big; it looks as if I swallowed a walnut and now it's just stuck there. There is a wad of cotton wool taped to my cheek, my lip is swollen to the size of a bowling ball and my right arm is bandaged all the way from the elbow to the wrist. I really do look as if I have been hit by a bus.

With a 'why worry' lift of my shoulders, I snatch up the zapper to turn on the TV.

'SIMON!' Dad calls up the stairs. 'A visitor for you. She's on her way up.'

A visitor! For me! AND IT'S A SHE! My thumb hovers over the TV 'On' button. But nobody ever visits me. Unless it's Granny Spittle armed with scissors and a comb. The 'Pat! Pat! Pat!' of footsteps, too fast to be Granny's and, a second later, Isabella is standing by my door.

Puzzled, I stand there and look at her.

'Do you plan to ask me in or is there a password?'

'Yes,' I say.

She frowns. 'Yes, you plan to ask me in or yes, there's a password?'

'Yes, there is a password.'

'I see. Is it Nerd?'

'No.'

'Geek?'

'No.'

'Is it, er...'

'No. Here's a clue. Spock was born there?'

'Glasgow?'

I roll my eyes. 'No.'

'Oh! I know. The planet Dweeb in the Nerd Galaxy.'

'Oh, forget it,' I say.

She shrugs and strolls in. Sorrowfully, I, in turn, drop the TV zapper on the bed.

I see she's no longer in her school uniform. Now she has on shorts, gold-buckled sandals and a long-sleeved jumper. She's also dyed her fringe indigo-blue, the rest of her curls bunched up on top of her skull like a candle wick.

'The cut on your lip looks pretty nasty,' she says.

I nod. 'I'll probably be scarred for life.'

'Hmm.' She turns away. 'Not a fun club to be in.'

She's never been in my room before and I feel a little jumpy; and when I'm jumpy, I say stupid stuff, so I blurt out, 'Your fringe is blue. Did you fall in a toilet?'

'No,' she retorts. 'I dyed it.' Twisting to look in my mirror, she puts her index finger to the scar on her cheek. 'It's my new look,' she says gloomily.

'The top looks like a candle wick,' I remark.

'Thanks Mop. I feel much better now.' Her eyes slowly wander my room. 'How is it you can be this tidy but you always look such a mess?'

'I don't like combs,' I tell her.

'Don't tell me,' she grins, 'they upset you.'

'Terribly,' I say with gravity.

Isabella rewards my sincerity with a wry smile. 'No fish bowl, I see.'

'No. I don't like fish. They drink where they pee.'

Nodding, she strolls by me and over to my shelf of Star Trek comics. I see there is a tiny speck of gravy on her top lip and she smells of lemon with just a slight whiff of...

'Your mum cooked you pork chops for dinner,' I tell her smugly.

With a thoughtful frown, she prods her lips with her tongue, finds the gravy and licks it off.

'Now for dessert. Hmm, let me think.' I tap my

chin with my index finger. 'There was lemon in it but what was the lemon in? Difficult. Difficult. I know! Curd. Lemon curd.'

'No, Sherlock, sorbet.'

'LEMON sorbet?'

She nods and rolls her eyes.

'And your dad dropped you here,' I tell her confidently.

'No, Mum did.'

'Ah ha! So you WERE dropped here?'

'Yes.'

'And she stopped at the Shell on the corner to fill up.'

'Yes, she did. How...'

'In fact,' I interrupt her, 'you filled up and she went in the shop to pay.'

Her eyes narrow to tiny slits. 'I'm not overly

keen on stalkers.'

'You smell of petrol,' I enlighten her smugly.

She sighs. 'Honestly, Mop, you so know how to sweep a girl off her feet.' She returns to browsing my shelf. 'You can always tell a person by the books they - Golly! What a lot of...'

'Star Trek comics, yes. Three hundred and sixty-seven. And I have two Star Trek uniforms in my drawer.'

'For Halloween?'

'No. Weddings and funerals.'

'Oh.' She nods slowly. 'You must look very er, smart.'

'I do,' I agree with her. 'If you ever want to borrow...'

'No. Honestly.' She grins. 'I'm good.' I watch the tips of her fingers brush the trumpet. 'So you do have a hobby.'

'Not really,' I say. 'It hurts my lips.' I do not want her to ask me to play. I'd only mess up: miss the F and play the G.

'And what's that up there? A frying pan?'

'No,' I say frostily, 'it is a model of the Starship Enterprise NCC-1701. I prefer it to the later ships. Admittedly, the NCC-1701-E is much sleeker, but the hull is way too thin. A direct hit from a Klingon Bird of Prey disruptor cannon and BOOM! Bits of trellium-D armour plating everywhere.'

'Wow! This Star Trek-thing is your life.' She frowns. 'You do know it's just a TV show, right? Klingons, they don't exist.'

'Do they not? Well, Miss Clever Clogs, did you know astronomers think, this galaxy, the Milky

Way, has possibly 4,000,000,000 planets in it?'

The corners of Isabella's lips twitch up. 'No,' she says, 'I did not know that.'

'And the Milky Way is just a tiny galaxy in a universe full of them. 176,000,000,000, according to the Hubble telescope.'

'Golly.'

'A little arithmetic - well, for you, a lot..'

'Mop!'

'...will tell you, then, that there must be over seventy zero zero zero zero zero zero zero zero zero zero zero zero zero zero zero zero zero zero zero zero zero planets in the universe. That's twenty-one zeros, by the way. With so many planets, anybody who tells you there's no other intelligent life in the universe is full of, er...'

'Poo?'

'Correct.'

'Hmm.' Isabella nods slowly. 'So why don't lots of little green men drop in and say hello?'

'The closest galaxy is 2,500,000 light years away. So, if they travelled at the speed of light, they'd get here in...'

'2,500,000 years.'

'Correct!' I look to her and arch my left eyebrow. I'm very good at it. I copy Spock off Star Trek; he's the king of eyebrow arching.

Isabella puckers up her lips. 'You know, I can multiply - by 1 anyway.'

I nod absentmindedly. 'To travel such a long way, they'd need to be highly intelligent; so intelligent you and I, everybody on this planet, we'd be just goldfish to them. Why bother to travel 2,500,000 light years to chat to goldfish?'

'You know, I see your lips moving but the only thing coming out is blah, blah, blah.'

I ignore her and stretch up my hand for the starship model. 'Here. You can play with it if you want to.'

'Oh, er - no thanks,' she says, back-pedalling.

'But it's battery-powered. It can shoot a photon torpedo 17.2 feet.'

'Mop, how can I put this gently? I'd rather chew off my legs, crawl through the Sahara Desert, strap rocks to my bloody stumps and drown myself in the River Nile.' She looks over at my bed. 'Is there a cuddly hen on your pillow?'

'Yes. From my granny. Why?'

'Oh, I just wondered, you know...'

'No.'

'Well, it's just I can't see anybody excitedly ripping open a present, and yelling, 'Oh, goody! It's a stuffed hen.'

'I love my hen,' I tell her stiffly. 'I call her Kentucky. She helps me to sleep.'

'Good,' she says. 'Very, very er - good.' It seems Isabella is a little lost for words. Astonishing! But she soon recovers. 'It's odd, don't you think? You're so clever, you know so much, but you still sleep with a stuffed hen on your pillow.'

I grunt and shrug my shoulders. 'Beethoven slept with a fluffy pig.'

I follow her over to the window and, there, I show her my Gypsy Boy rose.

'Wow! It's a whopper. What you been feeding it? Big Macs?'

I Think I Murdered Miss

I'm 99.9% positive she's being sarcastic. She must know you can't feed flowers beef burgers. So I say nothing and show her my watering can.

'Then you must talk to it a lot,' she asserts. 'My grandad told me, if you chat to flowers, they grow faster.'

'No, they don't.'

'Yes, they do. Music helps too. His tulips particularly enjoy Elvis.'

'That's stupid.'

'No, it's not.'

'Yes, it is. Look, you can agree with me or you can be wrong. It's up to you.'

She steps up to me, her fists on her hips. 'So you think my hundred and two year old grandad is a big, fat fibber?'

Startled, I back away. 'No, I er...'

Her lips tilt up and she winks at me. 'I'm just messing with you. My grandad's totally do-lally. He thinks there's a monster in his kettle. Anyway, all I can say is, your fingers must be very green to grow such a tall flower. And, yes, I know, nobody's got green fingers. It's just a saying.'

'Actually, the Hulk's got green fingers,' I inform her matter-of-factly. I screw up my nose in thought. 'But I don't think he's much of a gardener.'

Isabella's chin abruptly drops to her chest. 'Mop! Did you just tell a joke?'

'No.' I pucker up my brow. 'But if I did, why didn't you laugh?'

'Well, it wasn't very funny, was it?' With a giggle - now I'm totally confused - she picks up the photograph. 'Is this your mum?'

'Yes.'

'She's pretty.'

'Is she?'

'Yes.' She puts a fingertip to my mum's oval face. 'Every mum's pretty.'

This is obviously not correct. Borris, a boy six doors down, has a mum the size of a hippo - seventeen chins and I suspect a strong supporter of Mars Bar-sponsored slimming - but before I can tell her all this, she asks, 'What happened to her?'

'Skin cancer,' I mutter, a bristly ball of hurt landing in my stomach with a jolt.

'Oh. I'm sorry.' The hint of a frown creeps over her brow. It picks up speed and she begins to chew briskly on her top lip. 'In er, school today, when you warned me to stay out of the sun and I, er...'

'Belittled me? Put me down? Took the...'

'Yes. That.' I watch her hop from foot to foot. 'Well, I didn't know, you know...'

'No.'

She sighs. 'Mop, you're not helping.'

'I'm not?'

She sighs even deeper. 'I didn't know skin cancer killed your mum.'

'Oh. OK.'

'I'm sorry if I upset you. Did I?'

'No.'

'Good.' Gently, she puts the photograph down. 'Do you remember her?'

'She only left Dad and I four months, three weeks, two days and,' I check my watch, 'sixteen hours ago. The very day you moved here. So, yes, I remember her. I remember her smell anyway.'

'Did she smell of flowers? Oh!' Her mouth drops open, 'Is that why you keep a rose in your bedroom? To remind you of her?'

'No. She was a vet. She smelt mostly of wet dog.'

She titters. Then stops. 'Not a joke?'

'No.'

She nods. 'I thought not.' Then she digs in her bag and pulls out a ruler wrapped in a red ribbon and crowned with a bow. 'Here.' She hands it to me. 'A present.'

I study it with interest. 'This is a Star Trek ruler,' I tell her. 'The ruler Anthony snapped in two was a Star Wars.'

'Is it different then?'

I look to her in total and utter astonishment. 'Different! DIFFERENT! Is Newton's theory of gravity different to Einstein's?'

She frowns and thoughtfully rubs her chin with her finger and thumb.

'OK, not a good example. Is a Skoda different to a Ferrari then? Or a Picasso different to a six year old's felt tip sketch of her mum and her dad under a wonky, yellow sun? Or is a...'

'OK! OK! I get it. Keep your er, y-fronts on. Star Trek is different to Star Wars. And Star Trek is better. Yes?'

'Yes. Much.'

'So you must be happy with the ruler then.'

'Yes. Very.'

With Star Trek's honour nobly defended, I

return to studying my gift.

'Don't forget to say the all important word.'

I frown thoughtfully. 'But there must be hundreds of them,' I protest. My eyes shift up and left. "Atom' is a very important word and so is 'proton' and 'electron' and...'

'Thanks.'

'What for?'

She sighs. 'No, you say 'thanks' to me.'

'Oh!' I nod. 'But 'Atom' is a very important...'

'Mop!'

'Thank you. But no hugs,' I add, taking a precautionary step back. 'I'm not a big...'

'Hugger. Yes, surprisingly, I know. It's all the tiny, tiny hints.'

I scowl. I think - yes, she is, she's mocking me. I can tell.

Isabella curls her back, puts her nose up to a flower bud and sniffs.

I know the other kids in school think she's a bit of a rebel. They often tell me how trendy she is and how funny, and I know most of the boys think she's pretty. Even the scar on her cheek looks cool, though I think it helps that she tells everybody she got bitten by a crocodile.

'Why do you hang out with me?' I suddenly blurt out.

'You helped me with my maths homework.'

'Algebra,' I remind her, 'and I still do.'

She nods, straightening her back. 'Yes, you do.' She seems to ponder me for a moment; the seconds tick by and I begin to feel like a bug under a magnifying glass. I don't like it when people look at me. 'I think you're different,' she suddenly says. 'Interesting. I like you.'

Now, I think, must be the perfect moment to smile, so I do. With gusto!

'Oh,' she looks a little flustered and her cheeks burn crimson, 'but not in that way.'

'What way?'

'You know. That way.'

'Oh.' I finally get it. That way.

Gently, reverently, I put the ruler down on the window sill. Then I pick up the watering can and begin to water my flower. 'Dad told me a joke yesterday,' I tell her. 'About this Irishman who spent twelve hours trying to drown a fish.'

Isabella snorts. 'Now that's funny.'

'It reminded me of my life.' I look up at her. 'You know, it's difficult to be me; the way I am.'

'I bet,' she says softly.

'Every day, when I go to school or to the shop or, well, anywhere to be honest, I always screw up. Always.'

'Not always, Simon.' She never calls me Simon. 'Not with me.'

'But I do. Right now, this very second, there is a smile on your face. But I don't know why. Is it a happy smile, a wicked smile, or just a sad smile? Yesterday, in the lunch queue, you arched your eyebrow and I thought, yes, I know why, she's just seen the humongous pile of chips on Polly Smith's tray. But, no, you just had a bit of dirt in your eye.'

'To tell the truth, Polly trumped. It was terrible.'

'You see! Never even crossed my mind.'

'Noooo! Honestly? But it was soooo eggy.'

'Then there's sarcasm. Sarcasm to me is like an A grade in maths to you. A total and utter unknown.'

'Gee, thanks.'

'Anyway, what I'm trying to say is when I try to GET you, or dad, or Mrs Radinski in the Spar, it reminds me of trying to drown fish. Totally and utterly impossible.'

There is another roll of thunder and, a little red-faced by my sudden turn of honesty, I look out of the window to the garden below. The flower beds seem to be drowning in green: strangled with brambles and choked with weeds. The grass too is overgrown and pitted with clumps of moss. The mower, I know, is in the corner of the tool shed, hidden in a velvety blanket of cobwebs and dirt. But Dad's not big on gardening. Not now. Not now Mum's not here.

An evil-looking thunder cloud is slowly invading the sky and it is beginning to get awfully gloomy out. A lamp on the street seems to agree with me and flickers on. Instantly, I spot a boy lurking just under it. It is the new boy and, to my surprise, he is looking right back up at me.

'What's up?' asks Isabella, stepping closer. Instinctively, I shift ever so slightly to my right.

'There's...OH! He's not there now. There's just a ginger cat.'

'Who?' She cocks her head like a wary sparrow. 'Who's not there?'

'The new boy; I don't know his name, but he's scrawny and his skin looks sort of - papery. He only started today.'

'Felix,' she says softly.

'Yes. Yes, Felix.' I arch my eyebrow. I'm a little surprised she knows. 'I think I saw him by the streetlamp out there.'

'Well, did you or didn't you?' She seems oddly upset.

'I did,' I say.

'Turn off the light.'

'Why?'

'Just do it, Mop.'

I shrug and, with the watering can still clutched in my fist, I trot over to my desk and switch off the lamp.

I turn back to see her grip hold of the bottom of the window and wrench it up. Then she unzips her bag and slips her hand in it.

'Can you see him?' I whisper, clumping back over.

'No, I can't,' she says slowly.

I don't know why Felix spooked me so much. It is only six o'clock in the evening so it is hardly newsworthy to see a boy on the street. Now I think of it, No. 662, two doors down, did just sell. I bet Felix and his family moved in there. But he did spook me. And, if I'm honest, I do know why. It was his eyes. They were so golden. So...

Creepy!

And they were focused totally and utterly on me.

I look nervously at Isabella who is by my elbow. She is frowning deeply, her darting eyes still on the street below. She looks, I think, much taller than I remember and considerably older than her eleven years. I spot her hand is still hidden in her bag and I wonder what she has in there.

Abruptly, she slams the window shut with such a 'BANG!', the glass cracks and I drop the watering can on my foot. 'Let's go!' she snaps.

'GO!' I look to her in horror; difficult to do when I'm hopping up and down clutching my throbbing toe. 'I can't just go. There's too much to do.'

Felix is now totally forgotten, wiped from my mind by the thought of missing six hours of Kirk and his intrepid crew in yellow Spandex uniforms, phasers on stun, battling green, toothy monsters.

'Mop, there's nothing to do. Not in here anyway, unless you enjoy playing with dolls.'

'Dolls! DOLLS! A baby plays with dolls.' I pick up Spock and wave it in her face. 'This here happens to be a fully-working model of Spock, born 2030 in the city of Shi'Kahr on the planet Vulcan...'

'Oh!' She snaps her fingers. 'So the password to your room is Vulcan.'

I ignore her. 'Son of Ambassador Sarik, half brother to Sybok...'

'Who's his mum?'

I scowl. 'I'm sorry, who's his...'

'Mum, yes. Who's his mum?'

'Is it relevant?'

'Yes.'

'I don't see how.'

'It is.'

'Well, I don't see how.'

'Well, it is.'

I eye her sceptically. 'Amanda,' I mutter.

'Amanda. AMANDA! Not very exciting, is it? There's Spock, Shi'Kahr, Sillybook...'

'Sybok,' I hiss.

'Yes, yes, Sillybook; and then there's Amanda. It's so dull.' She scans my shelf. 'And, anyway, where's her doll?'

'There is no doll, er - model, of her.'

'How sexist.'

'Star Trek is not...'

'Whatever. Now, let's go.'

'But, but,' my eyes dart to my alarm clock, 'Star Trek's on. Six hours of it. It starts with episode eighteen where Spock mind-melds with a Gorn, a twenty-seven limbed monster from the planet Althos IV in the Chin'tok system. I can't possibly miss it. Not all of it.'

Isabella nods slowly. 'Six hours of Star Trek. I

can hardly control myself.'

Wonderful! I spiked her interest. I will try to convert her...

'Interesting monster, the Gorn. Admittedly, he looks a lot like a gigantic lump of elephant poo but if you can just get by that...'

'Just shut up and follow me.' Her eyes hard and uncompromising.

'But - the Gorn!'

'Just do it, Mop. OK?'

'No!' I cry. I will not let her bully me.

'Fine! But think on this, if Anthony's hit by a bus, every kid in school will think you murdered him.' She steps up to me, the two-foot rule forgotten. 'With your mind!'

I deflate like an old tyre. I don't want to be put in a loony asylum. Dad needs me too much.

I Think I Murdered Miss

Chewing fretfully on my bottom lip, I snatch my music player up off the bed and hook it on my belt. 'Where we off to then?' I say grumpily.

'I seem to remember you telling me you had an IQ of over a hundred and fifty.' She pulls a Kit Kat from her bag and strolls over to the door. 'So you work it out, Mr Clever Clogs.'

For a second, I stand there, cradling Dr. Spock in my hands. Then I sit him softly on the window sill between my new ruler and my Gypsy Boy rose. 'Don't let her upset you,' I tell the three of them. Then, with a wistful look at my TV set, I do up the only button still left on my cardigan and limp from the room.

Chapter 6

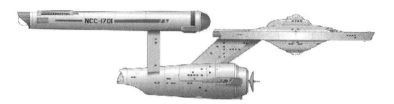

CURLY-TIPPED, STRIPY-LACED BOOTS

DRAGGING MY FEET, I FOLLOW ISABELLA BY THE tool shed and up the path to the street. There, by the gate, she stops.

There is a 'TAP! TAP! TAP!' and I look over my shoulder to spot my dad in the kitchen window. He is grinning insanely and giving me the thumbs up.

'He's very sweet, your dad,' Isabella says.

I snort uncommittedly. 'He's just excited I'm off to the circus. On a Star Trek night,' I add. 'With a girl.'

Isabella tuts. 'Oh! Bless!' And flutters a hand at him. Then, from nowhere, she asks me, 'How do you want to travel there? On foot or by bus?'

For a second, I just look at her. The big top is all the way down by the river at the bottom of Scar Hill, an awfully long way from here, but there's no way I'm getting on a bus. Any bus. Ever.

'Just kidding,' she laughs and, with a wink, she strolls off.

'This is crazy,' I mutter, pulling up a sock till it's perfectly level with the other. Then, watchful for cracks in the path, I run (and hop) to catch her up.

Under the swollen belly of the thunder cloud, we trudge up Warts Way. Then we turn left by the Spar. I spot Mrs Radinski in the window and smile manically at her. 'Just shutting,' she mouths, scuttling over to the door and locking it.

'Another fan of yours?' murmurs Isabella.

'No,' I say with a sigh, 'and she's no fan of Star Trek.'

'Well, she's just a crazy lady. Lock her up, I say.'

I nod my agreement. 'Anyway, I think my smile was too, er - big.'

'Did you just win the lottery?

'No.'

'Did you just find the legendary Lost City of Gold?'

'No.'

I Think I Murdered Miss

'Then, yes. It was.'

As we walk, Isabella hardly says a word and keeps looking over her shoulder. I suspect she thinks Felix is following us. I wonder idly why he's put her so much on edge; so on edge, she cracked my bedroom window, but when I try to bring it up she just turns all melodramatic and says darkly, 'Don't pry. I can't tell you.'

I attempt to look for him too, but all I see is a stray cat with a limp and a man by a shed with a barrow full of dirty turnips.

Eventually, I switch on my music to listen to Art Tatum. He was a black American born in 1909. A jazz player. A pioneer. An improviser. In fact, everything I'm not. I often wonder if that is why I enjoy his music so much. I do try to play jazz on my trumpet but I'm all thumbs and Mrs

Cherry keeps hammering on the wall. Then, when she sees me, she always says, 'Y'd scare off a ruddy elephant with all y' racket.'

Turning right by the town hall, I enjoy the soothing harmony of 'Makin' Whoopee'. Then, by the tennis ball factory, the messy, totally crazy, totally over-the-top 'Tiger Rag'.

The stink of rubber from the works sweeps over me and I tweezer my nostrils in my fingers. My nose is, to put it mildly, super powerful. I smell everything. EVERYTHING! If I was a superhero, I'd be Supersniffer or Supersmelly - oh, not so good - or, I know, Wonder Whiff! Hmm. Wonder Whiff. Pretty cool.

At last, all hot and sticky from the walk, we plod over the crest of Scar Hill. And, there, we see it: Billy Smart's Circus big top, the red and yellow striped awning billowing gently in the breeze. It is nesting on the bank of the river in amongst a labyrinth of wooden stalls, merry-go-rounds and old, rusty Volvos. A lorry with a poster of an elephant on the driver's door sits in the shadow of the helter-skelter and, just next to it, I spot a big, red double-decker bus.

With a dry mouth, I fumble with the off-button on my music player.

Even from up here it looks terrifying. All bold and blood red. A TOWERING MONSTER! Even the grill on the front reminds me of a snarling dog's teeth. A growl of thunder booms over the town, so perfectly matching the moment, I wonder, for a second, if I'm in a horror film.

'That must be the bus that hit Miss Belcher,' Isabella says.

Speechless, I muster a tiny nod. It's as if my jaw's been wired shut.

We trot down the hill. Then, when we get to the first of the stalls: a hoopla stall with stuffed bunny rabbits and wooden toy cars hooked in the roof, we slow to a walk. The grass is very uneven, strewn with paper cups and sweet wrappers and pitted with muddy ruts.

'I detest paper cups,' I whisper.

Isabella titters. 'Chin up, Mop. I don't see any parrots.'

'Oh good,' I mutter, my shoulders slumped. 'I forgot to bring nuts.'

Warily, we work our way between a coconut shy and a woman with shockingly pink lips and a shockingly pink scarf selling shockingly pink candyfloss. Then, finally, we creep over to the

KILLER BUS

But for the candyfloss lady, there's nobody about, 'Ooohs!' echoing from the big top not twenty feet away. It is, I see, looking a little old and worn, a patch here and there peeling off like the skin of a potato; the rope holding it up greened with moss and ragged and splayed at the ends.

'The show must still be on,' murmurs Isabella.

'Anthony must be in there,' I reply.

She nods, her fingers curling and uncurling on the strap of her bag. Then she says, in a very 'boding evil' sort of way, 'Unless he got hit by a different bus on the way here.'

'Isabella!' I stop by the front wheel of the

double-decker and, with fists on hips, I turn to her. 'Miss Belcher was accidentally hit by a bus. The important word there is, accidentally. It wasn't witchcraft; and I will tell you why. Witchcraft only happens in books and films. Fantasy books and films. The important word there is, fantasy.'

'Wizardry, not witchcraft,' she corrects me. 'Remember, you're a boy.'

I feel my jaw harden. There is a fist under my rib cage, clawing and pummelling, looking for a way out.

With a look of alarm, Isabella steps back. 'Don't start kicking stuff, will you.'

'No,' I seethe, my mood volcanic, 'I won't. Not if you listen to...'

'I got it!' She snaps her fingers, silencing me.

'Let's let a tyre down on the bus. No! Even better. All four of them.'

Stunned, my jaw drops open, warning bells ringing in my ears.

Isabella begins to pace, chomping thoughtfully on her lower lip. 'Then, when the circus is over, there's no way Anthony can get hit by it.' She looks over at the big top. 'But we must hurry. The show will probably be over soon. Keep a look out.'

Totally wrong-footed, I try to protest. 'But the candyfloss lady, she'll spot us.' But Isabella's already dropped to a knee and I watch, nervously, as she starts to unscrew the dust cap.

It is odd how, with just a snap of her fingers, this girl can cool my temper. I remember, when I was much younger, how my mum simply hugged me till I stopped yelling. That always worked too. But Isabella's not my mum. She's not even my big sister. So what, I wonder, is she.

'You know, I can't spend every hour of every day following Anthony everywhere,' I tell the crown of her skull. 'He'll think I want to mug him.'

'No, he won't. He'll just think you fancy him.'

'FANCY HIM! But, but...'

'There's that 'but' word. Twice. Honestly, Mop, if you keep this up, you'll soon be normal; you'll want to kick footballs and run everywhere.'

'But, but...'

'That's four,' she says, and with a final twist of the dust cap, it pops off.

'I, I don't fancy him,' I bluster. 'I'm not, you know...'

'Loosen up, Mop. I'm just messing with you.'

I balloon my cheeks. 'Well, stop it. It's off-putting.'

She lifts her chin and grins up at me. 'Anyway, if you did put a spell or a hex or whatever it was on him...'

'I DID NOT PUT A...'

'...it will only last for a day or two.'

My eyes widen and I glower back down at her. 'A day or two! How can you possibly know that?'

She shrugs and drops the dust cap in the grass. 'Just a wild guess.'

'Oy! You two!' I look up to see, not the candyfloss lady, but a tubby man in mud-splattered overalls clomping over to us. 'What y' up to there?' he growls, sipping Coke and belching savagely.

'I was er, just doing up my lace,' Isabella says, jumping to her feet.

The man scowls and, with a twitch of his eye, rubs his soft buttery chin. 'But y' got sandals on.'

'Yes, I do,' says Isabella matter-of-factly. 'Did I say lace?'

'Yep,' says the man.

'You did,' I volunteer with a concurring nod.

Isabella attempts to shut me up - well, I think so anyway - with a frosty look and a deep furrow of her brow. She turns back to the man. 'Sorry,' she tweets, smiling sweetly up at him. 'My buckle. I was doing my buckle up.'

The man snorts. His eye, I see, is still twitching. 'Ay, well, whatever y' up to, just keep away from this 'ere bus. There's been coppers 'ere all day fiddling with it, trying to work out if the steering's dodgy or not. You see, yesterday, it murdered a woman.'

A chill creeps from the bottom of my feet all the way up to the roots of my curls. 'Murdered,' I echo him. Isabella and I look at each other. 'A bus can't murder.'

'Well, my old pal, Jimmy, thinks differently. He was driving the brute and he told me, his words, 'The wheel just turned.' Went for her, it did. Got the devil in, Jimmy reckons.' He kicks the bumper. Then, promptly, he steps away, as if frightened the bus might kick him back.

Together, we watch him stomp over to the candyfloss lady.

'So it WAS magic,' says Isabella. Slowly, she swivels on her heels to look at me. 'You did hex her.'

I scowl back mulishly, stiffening my knees. 'Rubbish!' I utter back. 'Jimmy, whoever he is, probably fell asleep at the wheel.' Then I drop my eyes to my feet; I do not want her to see how the man's words had unsettled me, flooding my stomach with acid. 'Well, anyway, it was a good try,' I say bracingly. 'So, Star Trek it is. If we hurry, we can catch the last two hours.'

But Isabella, it seems, is in no mood to throw in the towel just yet and with a perfunctory, 'Follow me', she strolls over to the back corner of the bus. With iron-filled boots, I trudge doggedly after her. Just by the bumper, dwarfed by the big top, there is another tent. It is octagonal-shaped and there is a yellow flag fluttering on the top. Isabella creeps over to it and lifts the flap. Then, with a beckoning finger, she slips in.

I do not want to follow her but there is a low throbbing growl and I suspect, directly over me, hidden by cloud, there is a plane. A month ago, I watched a documentary on the Discovery Channel called 'Best Not To Ask' and was shocked to find out that when passengers go to the loo at 30,000 feet, the poo and wee is simply flushed out. And now I keep imagining parachuting poo.

With this in mind, I cower under my hands and dash after her.

Once in the tent and safe from any plummeting terds, I discover Isabella perched on a stool powdering her cheeks. By her knees there is a low bench with a chipped mirror bolted to the top. A box of lipsticks sits just in front of it along with three curly, poppy-red wigs. Over in the corner, there is a wardrobe, the door wide open to display a shelf of crumpled-up, fluffy-cuffed shirts and, on the shelf below, a messy hill of curly-tipped, stripy-laced boots.

'This is where the clowns must dress,' says Isabella.

I nod, warily. 'Yes,' I reply.

'Well, I just thought of the most brill' plan.'

'Now there's a shocker,' I murmur, letting my bottom fall onto the corner of the bench. 'And stop shortening your words; or do you need to rush off to the...'

'No,' she growls. 'I don't need the loo.'

I shrug and screw up my nose. The tent stinks of B.O. and dirty socks with a hefty topping of fatty food. The culprit, I see, sits just by me: a 'munched-on' McDonald's triple-burger and three ketchup-drowned chips.

Messy fellows, clowns; and I wonder if it'd be OK if I tidy up a bit.

'Let's dress up too,' says Isabella, excitedly. 'Then everybody will think we work here and nobody will try to stop us when we let the tyre down on the bus.' She picks up a wig and puts it on. 'What do you think? Do I look stupid?'

'Yes,' I tell her. 'Very. You look like a Red Setter.'

She eyes me coldly then twists back to the mirror to apply cherry lipstick to her cheeks.

'There is, I think, just a tiny, tiny problem with your, er - can I call it a plan?'

'Do tell,' she snaps. I think the Red Setter

comment upset her.

'The job of a clown is to throw stuff, trip over, jump on a unicycle and juggle frying pans. It is not a clown's job to let down the tyre on a bus. So, we will still look a little suspect, don't you think?'

'Oh.' For a moment, she looks crestfallen. Then, 'I know,' her chin lifting, 'if anybody asks, we can tell them we ran out of puff and we need to fill our balloons.'

'Fill - our - balloons!' I say this very, very slowly.

She nods enthusiastically. 'Yep. From the tyre.'

I look to her in total and utter bewilderment. How can anybody think up such a dumb plan? It's bewildering. It's so bewildering I'm almost speechless. Almost…

'That must be the most stupid plan in the history of stupid plans,' I tell her. 'Even compared to George Lucas' plan to put Jar Jar Binks in a Star Wars film or Custard's last stand at Little Big Horn.'

'Hey?'

'IT WON'T WORK, ISABELLA!'

Isabella screws up her lips. 'So what's your super plan, IQ Boy?'

I scowl and rub my eyes. I can't think of any.

Grudgingly, I dab powder on my face and blotch my cheeks with lipstick. I pull on a pink, flowery shirt, big-bottomed shorts and curly-tipped, stripy-laced boots. Then I bury my wiry, skew-whiff curls under the curls of a red wig.

'You look better in the wig,' says Isabella.

I grunt and tell her to hurry up. But when I look over, I see she's all set to go. Dressed in shiny polkadot shorts and curly boots, she too looks perfectly clownish. She's even slipped a plastic sunflower in the button hole of her fluffy-cuffed shirt.

'It squirts water,' she tells me, her eyes twinkling. She puts her hand in her pocket and, a split second later, a jet of water erupts from the flower, drenching my shorts.

'MOP!' she hoots, waggling a finger in the vicinity of my zipper. 'Did you wee your y-fronts?'

'Ha, ha,' I mutter.

I stuff my music player under the bench with Isabella's bag. Then, together, we slip out of the tent.

I Think I Murdered Miss

The wind has picked up, whipping up the sweet wrappers and the paper cups and playing havoc with the candyfloss lady's pink scarf. Screening my eyes, I peer over at the big top and there, by the flapping door, I spot a crowd of circus performers.

Silver-wrapped tumblers, jugglers on stilts, and clowns; lots and lots of clowns: plump, skinny, a clown on a unicycle and a clown with a bucket and a bowl of wobbly jelly. There is even a herd of zebras, a dour-looking pony - he reminds me a bit of Eeyore in Winnie the Pooh - and an elephant with a tassled rug draped over his back.

Towering over them - well, most of them, not the elephant or the fellows on the stilts - is a portly man with a gold-tipped baton in his fist.

Waterfalls of fat seep from under his sparkly tunic and a perfectly trimmed, curly-tipped moustache sits on his top lip. He must be the ringmaster.

Suddenly, he spots us. 'OY! YOU TWO!' he bellows, waving us over with his stick.

I look at Isabella but she just shrugs. So, reluctantly, we plod over to the big top and stand with the rest of the performers.

'What a truly wonderful plan this is,' I whisper crossly.

'Just play the clown,' Isabella growls back.

'Play the clown!' I hiss, the words whipped from my lips by the squalling wind. 'I have the IQ of a chemistry professor, I don't PLAY the clown. Anyway,' I shrug, 'I don't know how to.'

'Yes you do. You just told me back in the

clowns' tent. Throw stuff, trip over, jump on a unicycle and...'

'Juggle frying pans. Yes, yes, I know. But what I don't know is HOW TO!'

'Hush!' the clown by my elbow scolds me.

'Wonderful show, everybody,' booms the ringmaster. 'But now it is time for the big finale. Let's keep the energy up and end the night BIG!'

It is beginning to bucket it down, fat wet drops exploding off the walls of the tent and showering the huddled performers. There is another growl of thunder. The elephant, in an angry fit, stamps his foot and trumpets wildly back.

'Let's go,' carps a burly-looking acrobat in a pink, lacy leotard, who is standing on his hands. 'My bum's getting drenched.'

'TOP BUTTONS UP!' bellows the ringmaster.

'JUGGLERS JUGGLE! Oh, and Bobby.' He looks to the clown with the jelly. 'Try not to hit the crowd. You know how upset they get.'

Bobby nods. 'No problem, Boss.'

'Good. In we go then.' And, with a twirl of his baton, he stomps off.

To the playful whoops of the clowns and the trumpets and drums of the circus band, the troop of performers trot, march and cartwheel into the big top. Urgently, I try to elbow my way free, but I'm blocked in by a juggler's stilts and the stripy rump of a zebra. Isabella, to my left, is blocked in too, but by a considerably bigger obstacle: the swaying bottom of a twelve foot tall African elephant.

'I - I can't go in there,' I stutter.

'Just chill, Mop, And try not to walk like a

robot. Remember, y' a clown.'

'But this is how I walk.'

'I know. Stop it.'

'I can't just - stop it,' I mutter crossly.

Isabella sighs. 'When nobody's looking, we'll slip out of the big top and over to the bus.'

'When nobody's looking,' I hiss. 'WHEN NOBODY'S LOOKING! HELLO! We're clowns in a circus. Who's NOT going to be looking!?'

Just then, Bobby the clown stuffs a bucket of eggs in my hand. 'Try not to hit the crowd,' he tells me.

Numbly, I nod. It seems I must 'play the clown' after all.

Chapter 7

GRANNY'S TEETH

CRADLING THE BUCKET OF EGGS IN MY CLAMMY hands, I plod into the circus ring. Everywhere I look, I see cartwheeling acrobats and jugglers tossing up bowling pins and sharp-toothed saws. The herd of zebras gallop by, kicking up sawdust and the elephant trumpets and sits on a wooden ball.

With wobbly knees, I stand there. I just - stand there. I feel horribly boxed in, cut off from my sheltered world of Star Trek and chess. Hundreds of kids, mums and dads cheer and clap, all of them, ALL OF THEM staring at me. The fist in my chest is back, hammering relentlessly on my ribcage. I try to wet my lips but my tongue is too puffed up and dry.

Then, from out of nowhere, Isabella steps up to me, winks, and slams a custard tart in my face.

The crowd howls with laughter.

'Not funny,' I mutter, mopping drippy yellow goo off my chin. Then, with uncharacteristic relish, I put my hand in my bucket and splatter her with eggs.

It is at this very moment, at 7.37 on a thundery Wednesday night, that the oddest thing happens. So odd, it's not happened to me in four months, three weeks, two days and - I check my watch - seventeen hours.

I laugh.

And not just a giggly 'knock, knock, who's there' sort of laugh, but a chest-rattling belter of a laugh, an 'OH! Look! Granny's teeth fell in her soup' sort of laugh.

And I can't stop.

Scooping egg yolk off her eyelids, Isabella begins to laugh too. 'Look,' she says, 'I'm an omelette.' And she's still laughing when Bobby, the clown, lobs his strawberry jelly at me.

THIS IS WAR!

And, with a wild banshee cry, I machine gun

him with six eggs in a row. He ducks and they hit a boy in the crowd. Wiping a splodge of jelly off my cheek, I spot the unlucky boy is Anthony.

'ISABELLA!' I holler over the blaring trumpets of the circus band. 'LOOK! THERE HE IS!'

But Isabella, it seems, is not the slightest bit interested. In fact, she's not even looking at me; she's looking past me and by the way she's clenching and unclenching her fists and the set of her deeply arched eyebrows, I think she just spotted the devil. That or, remembering my error in the lunch queue, the elephant trumped.

I look over my shoulder and, instantly, I spy Felix in the crowd. He hops up from his bench and starts to walk over to us.

'MY BAG!' yells Isabella, hurrying over to me. 'Where is it?'

'Two-foot rule,' I remind her sternly.

'MOP! TELL ME!' she bawls, gripping hold of my shirt and shaking me.

Taken aback, I mutter, 'I think you left it under the bench in the clowns' tent.'

'I left it under the...' She stops and, with a jittery intake of breath, looks back at Felix. As thunder rolls over the big top, I look too. He is now only six feet away, standing there in the ring.

Just standing there.

Despite being a lot shorter than me and his tiny, wimpy-looking shoulders, he still frightens me. He puts me in mind of a sweet, fluffy kitten. With fangs!

He eyes Isabella keenly. She, stubbornly, returns his look.

'Is her blood in him?' he spits. 'Has he the gift?' He talks in such a way, it reminds me of rain pitter pattering on a tin roof.

'I don't know yet,' answers Isabella, letting go of my shirt and stepping in front of me. But I'm taller and I can still see.

Felix wets a fingertip and I spot his hands look all wrinkly as if he pickled them in a jar. Then, slowly, he pets his eyebrow. 'Fury will know,' he says softly as a tumbler cartwheels by, so softly I only just catch it. 'He will be here soon.'

'Sinjin Fury! Here?'

With a smirk - well, I think it's a smirk; maybe he's just smiling, happy to see us - he nods.

Feeling a bit of a third wheel, I ask, 'Who's Sinjin Fury?'

Felix's mouth drops open. 'Did sweet Izzy not

tell you?' He wags a long-nailed finger at her. 'Tut! Tut! Well, allow me to. Or, even better, I can show you...'

'Felix! No!' snarls Isabella.

But Felix just grunts, a sort of bullish snort. 'And who's going to stop me?' he sniggers.

Mesmerised, I watch him slip his hand in his pocket and...

'OY! You there!' The ringmaster storms over to Felix and taps him sharply on the shoulder with his baton. 'Back on your bench and let the clowns be. They got a job to do.'

Trying not to trip over her curly-tipped boots, Isabella turns to look at me. 'Let's go,' she whispers.

I look blankly back at her. 'Where to?'

'JUST RUN!' she howls.

I Think I Murdered Miss

The thunder storm, it seems, agrees with her, for, just then, a bolt of lightning hits the big top with a 'BANG!' and fire engulfs the canvas roof. The elephant trumpets and stamps his foot and everybody, even the clowns and the terribly depressed pony, bolt for the exit.

I want to be different, be the big hero and pull a tiny baby from the inferno, but, to be honest, I'm trying not to poop my y-fronts.

So I leg it too. I elbow and I kick. I trample and I barge. I even step on the slippered foot of an elderly man with a walking stick. Until, finally, huffing and puffing, I burst from the big top.

I skid to a stop by the candyfloss lady but, to my utter horror, Isabella is nowhere to be seen. With rain pummelling my cheeks, I look back at the tent. Most of the roof is ablaze, tiny fragments of glowing cloth twisting and twirling in the wind. Is she still in there, I wonder with a gulp. Trampled on in the stampede? The fire creeping up on her limp body?

'ISABELLA!' I holler, starting to wind my way back through the crowd.

'MOP! OVER HERE!'

I turn to see her hurrying over to me. The tip of her nose is all sooty and her flowery shirt is torn at the neck.

'Where were you?' I demand. I almost hug her. Then, I remember, I'm not much of a hugger.

'Sorry. This old man hurt his foot in the rush. A stupid clown stood on it. I stopped to help the poor fellow.'

'Oh!' I blush and drop my eyes to my curly-tipped feet. Truly sorry people look there. Dad told me.

'And I had to fetch this,' she adds, holding up her bag.

'Why?' I ask her sternly. 'What's in it that's so important? And what's up with you and this new boy, Felix? You act as if - as if he wants to kill us.'

'Kill us! No. He's not trying to kill us. He's trying to...'

A terrifying rumble cuts her off and we look over to see what's left of the big top's roof crash down. Sparks bellow up, drifting off over the town. Now only the wall is left, glowing wooden timbers peeping over the top of it. With the rest of the onlookers, we stand in the storm and watch the circus burn.

'I can't see Anthony,' mutters Isabella. She

begins to jump up and down, trying to see over the top of the crowd.

I drag my eyes from the inferno and hunt the throng for the bully's black, steely crew-cut. 'Nor can I,' I finally say.

All of a sudden, a woman in a grubby and torn spangly dress bursts from the big top. Coughing and rubbing the soot from her eyes, she staggers over to the crowd. 'Help me,' she pants. 'Bus is still in there.'

I feel Isabella's elbow in my ribs. 'Did she just say 'Bus'?' she whispers.

With panic welling up in my chest, I nod.

We watch two clowns hurry over to her. The plumper of the two puts his flowery tunic over her shoulders but she rips it off and grips him by the shirt. 'He's totally wild,' she bellows, 'and there's a kid trapped in there with him. A boy.'

A b-b-boy!' stutters the clown. 'There's a boy trapped in the big top with the elephant?'

With a feeble nod, she drops to her knees. 'Find the ringmaster,' she rasps. 'Now!'

Nodding stupidly, the two clowns hurry off.

Slowly, almost in a stupor, I turn to Isabella. 'The elephant's name is Bus,' I tell her. 'THE ELEPHANT'S NAME IS BUS!'

Isabella, however, seems totally unruffled by this world-shattering news. And, if I'm not mistaken: the hands on the hips, the tapping of the foot, she really, really, REALLY wants to say, 'I told you so.'

But no, she just says this, 'And I bet the boy is Anthony.'

My stomach twists. 'I think I'm gong to vomit,'

I croak. Am I a wizard, then? A dark wizard who can kill? With a wish? 'This can't be happening.' Bending over, I clutch my knees. 'It just can't.'

I feel Isabella's hand on my back but, this time, I do not pull away. 'I'm sorry, Mop,' she says, 'but it is.' Gripping my shoulders, she gently pulls me up. I see the red on her cheeks is blotched and her wig is sopping wet. 'Now, follow me,' she tells me sternly. 'We must try to help him.'

But the fire, I protest pathetically. 'I - I don't want to burn.'

Isabella scowls and chews on her bottom lip. 'This fellow, Kirk,' she suddenly says. 'He's the hero, yes? In Star Trek?'

'Yes,' I mumble.

'And he fights this Goon.'

I Think I Murdered Miss

'Gorn,' I correct her, 'from the planet Althos IV in the Chin'tok System.'

'I see. And this - Gorn, he's a terrifying monster, is he?'

'He's got twenty-seven legs.'

'Wow!' She grins. 'That's er - pretty terrifying. But I'm guessing Kirk faced him anyway.'

I clench my jaw and gulp, trying to swallow the wild terror rising up in me. I want to curl up in a ball, my cheeks to my knees, but I know she's right. Kirk and his bold crew of explorers never run away. Ever. Not even from a Gorn. 'I'm n-n-no hero,' I stumble, 'but I'll do my best.'

'I know you will.' She turns to go but, suddenly, she stops. 'Oh, and Mop, it's 'I will do my best' not 'I'll do my best'. Try to stop shortening your words.' She grins. 'Unless y' in a hurry and need

~ 161 ~

to rush off to the loo?' She twirls on her heels and sprints over to the big top.

I frown thoughtfully. I think - yes, yes, she did; the pretty girl with the low IQ just got the better of me. I sigh and with the Lord's prayer on my lips, I plod after her.

Chapter 8

A SHOWER OF SPELLS

WE HURRY INTO THE BIG TOP, ONLY TO BE engulfed by a swirling fog of of liquorice-black smoke. It floods my nostrils and stings my eyes and soon I cannot see a thing. With a babyish whimper, I tuck my hands in my armpits. I just want to be in my bed, Star Trek on the TV, Kentucky, my toy hen, curled up on my pillow, a cup of Cadbury's milk...

Suddenly, a hand grabs my knee, jolting me

back to the horrors of the burning tent. 'Drop low!' howls Isabella.

With a nervy gulp, I do as I'm told and, instantly, the smog thins. Rubbing my poor, tender eyes, I blink rapidly and look up. I'm met with the most horrifying sight. Even with much of the roof destroyed and the thunder storm still drenching the town, almost everything is burning. No. Scratch the 'almost'. Everything is burning. EVERYTHING! The tiered stands, the trapeze swings, even the pedals on a discarded unicycle and the elephant's wooden ball. Torn shreds of the tent's roof lay scorched and blackened in the sawdust and, over by the tent wall, a zebra trots in a circle and kicks his heels.

'Can you see Anthony anywhere?' puffs Isabella, who is hunkered down just next to me.

But I'm too busy eyeing the ball and wondering where Bus, the half-crazed elephant, is.

'Keep up!' barks Isabella and, stooping even lower, she runs off.

'This is ruddy nuts,' I mutter. For a second, I watch the trotting zebra. It must be very fulfilling, I think, to just run round and around. Then, trying not to trip over the trumpets and drums strewn in the sawdust, I chase after Isabella's scurrying heels.

We hurry by a tipped-up stool and a polkerdot yellow wheelbarrow, droplets of water hitting the hot steel with a hiss and a sputter. Even with the storm still over us, I feel hot and clammy and I tug violently on my shirt collar.

'LOOK!' yells Isabella. 'OVER THERE! I SEE HIM!'

Still bent over, we sprint - well, Isabella sprints, I lollop - over to where Anthony is lying slumped on the floor. He is whimpering softly and clutching his right foot. I spot there's a blob of egg yolk on his t-shirt. I must remember to tell him.

'Thank God,' he says when he sees us. 'I think I busted my ankle.' Then, feebly, 'I - I can't walk.'

'There's egg yolk on your t-shirt,' I inform him.

Isabella shoots me a look. 'It's OK,' she says, dropping to her knees and gently patting his shoulder. 'We will help you.' But Anthony's no longer listening. The big, scary bully's passed out.

'WE!' I protest, dropping to my knees too. My skin feels wet and prickly; it must be over a hundred degrees in here. 'But if I put my hands on him, I'll...'

'What?' growls Isabella. 'What will happen, Mop? Will you get the lergy? Will a Goon swallow you up?'

'Gorn,' I correct her feebly.

'Look!' She puts her hand on my knee. I scowl ferociously and she pulls it back. 'I'm not asking you to hug him. Just help me to carry him.'

'Carry him! CARRY HIM! And risk skin contact.' This is worse than I thought. 'I - I can - carry his hat.'

'His hat?'

'Yes.'

Isabella grits her teeth and mops her brow on the cuff of her shirt. 'He's not got a hat,' she snarls.

'Oh, you think so, do you? Well, Miss Know-It-All, what's that in the sawdust by his elbow?'

She turns to look. 'That,' she says with a long sigh, 'is a women's hat. You know, Mop, I often look at you and wonder, who's steering the ship.'

'It is not a women's hat," I say unwaveringly.

'Yes, it is.'

'IT - IS - NOT!'

'YES - IT - IS! It's pink, there's a pink ribbon on it - oh! And look, there's a pink flower pinned to the rim. It must be a women's hat.'

'ISABELLA! I'm shocked. And you had the cheek to call Star Trek sexist.'

'Mop! This is crazy.' She flaps her hands so frantically, her fingers ripple. 'Any second now the rest of this tent will topple over and we will be burnt to a crisp. And you - YOU want to discuss hats.'

'Pink is in, you know,' I say moodily. 'For men too. Anthony's mum probably lent it to him.'

'Mop!'

'Now, now, you two.' Almost magically, the smoke lifts and Felix strolls over. 'Let's not quarrel.'

'You!' spits Isabella, jumping deftly to her feet. She unzips her bag and slips her hand in it.

'Cool it, Izzy,' he says. 'There's no need for bloodshed.'

'There's every need, you slimy git.'

The boy backpedals two steps and licks his lips. Then his scarily-golden eyes find me. 'You know what Fury wants. He's not interested in you, Izzy. But he's very interested in Simon here.'

'Over my rotting body,' snarls Isabella. 'And stop calling me Izzy.'

Felix tuts and puts his hand in his trouser pocket. 'You know I'm better than you.' He sniggers. 'The scar on your cheek is proof of that. I'm much older too...'

She grunts. 'By a whopping two months,' she scoffs him.

He shrugs and his eyes narrow. 'Remember, I'm not shackled by the laws of your Sorcerer's Covern - or by silly regrets. Do the maths, IZZY, and step off.'

But she just grins. 'You know, Felix, and Mop will back me up on this, I'm not very good at maths.'

'She thinks a square root is a vegetable,' I concur with a vigorous nod.

I Think I Murdered Miss

Slowly, Isabella pulls a long, thin twig from her bag.

My shoulders sag. I was hoping for a shotgun. 'Er, what's that for?' I ask. Then I see Felix has a twig in his hand too.

'Mop!' snaps Isabella, her eyes still fixed on Felix. 'Help Anthony.'

But by now I'm beginning to get a bit annoyed by the two of them. 'You know, the big top's on fire,' I say stonily, 'and I'm still in it. Oh, and there's a very unhappy elephant in here too. So, drop your silly bits of wood and let's...'

A jet of powdery sparks erupt from the tip of Isabella's twig. No, not twig. WAND! They hit Felix in the stomach and, with a cry, he cartwheels to the floor.

'I got better,' Isabella says with a smirk.

Rubbing his belly, the boy clambers drunkenly to his feet. 'Rootify,' he yells. There is a 'BOOM!' and a tree root, twisting and jerking like a dying eel, hops out of the tip of his wand and begins to bind Isabella's legs together.

But, with a swish of her wand, she cuts the root in two. 'Much better,' she says evenly.

For a long, LONG moment Felix just glowers at her. Then, suddenly, he twirls on the spot and, a split-second later, he is - to put it simply - no longer there. Now, there is only a shabby-looking ginger cat.

With a hiss-like, 'MEOW!' it swings a paw at us then, limping slightly, it patters off, vanishing into the smoke.

'That's a new trick,' murmurs Isabella.

I look on in astonishment. 'Did he - did he

just...'

'Yes, he did,' says Isabella wryly.

'And you - did you just...'

She nods curtly and begins to walk off. 'Back in a sec.'

'Hey! Hold on!' I cry. 'Help me with Anthony.'

'Sorry, Mop. He's your problem now.' She puts a finger to her scarred cheek, her jaw hardening. 'The pig did this; butchered me, and I want him.' Then, she too, runs off.

'He's not a pig,' I mutter dazedly. 'He's a cat.'

So, I'm just left there, in Billy Smart's Circus big top, my mind aptly performing cartwheels, trying to get to grips with Felix being a wizard and Isabella, the girl I see every day at school, being a witch.

The fire is creeping ever closer, fed by the

sawdust on the floor. I glance at Anthony. He is still out for the count so, reluctantly, I yank down the sleeve of my flowery shirt until it covers my hand. Gripping hold of his uninjured left foot, I slowly begin to drag him over to the exit.

But then, with the flapping tent door in sight, the elephant trumpets.

Feeling as if a bucket of icy water has been thrown over me, I stop, my foot resting on the silvery metal of a discarded trumpet. I remember what the man with the twitch told us, how the bus swerved, mowing poor Miss Belcher down. Did I do that? Did my wish do that? And my second wish, for Anthony to be hit by a bus too, will this elephant, this elephant called Bus, carry it out? Will he bend to my will?

I know he's here, hidden in the swirling smoke.

Hunting us. Hunting Anthony. For a split second, I almost drop the boy's foot and run for it. But Isabella's words return to me. It is not the Star Trek way.

THUD! THUD! THUD!

I feel the sawdust under my feet shudder and, moments later, the elephant erupts from the smoke. With his javelin-like tusks level with my chest, it thunders over to us.

Dropping Anthony's leg to the scorched sawdust, I do the only thing I can think of. Remembering Mrs Cherry's words to me, 'Y'd scare off a ruddy elephant with all y' racket', I snatch up the trumpet from under my foot. It's so hot, I almost drop it. But, determinedly. I put it to my lips and blow.

And the elephant. It just stops. Stops. Just in

front of me, his long, wrinkly trunk dangling a foot from my nose.

Hastily pulling the trumpet from my scorched lips, I let it fall to the floor. Then, slowly, I look up. I'm met by the elephant's big, grey eyes.

With my knees knocking, I do what I always do when I'm frightened. I talk gibberish. 'A fossilised rose over 35,000,000 years old was discovered in the US,' I tell the towering monster. 'But the oldest living rose is in...' I trail off, a scowl slowly knotting my brow. There is a sort of cold, blank look to this elephant's eyes, empty, as if he'd been hypnotised.

With a waggle of his droopy lugs, he turns and lumbers off. In a befuddled daze, I watch him go.

Suddenly, a shadow erupts from the smoke and I jump back. But it is only Isabella, the wand still clutched in her fist.

'Your lips look very red,' she tells me.

'I burnt them playing the trumpet,' I reply. 'Three of my fingers too.' I show her.

She puts her fists on her hips. 'Mop, why were you playing the trumpet in a burning tent?'

'I was trying to frighten off the elephant?'

'Oh! Did it work?'

'Do you see the elephant?'

'No.'

'Then, yes, it did.'

She looks at me for a moment, her eyes narrow and thoughtful. Then, with a sigh, she looks down at Anthony. 'He's still out cold, I see.'

'You - you can do magic,' I splutter.

'Mop, I know a lot's happened and I know this is difficult for you, but not now, OK?'

I muster a jerky sort of nod. Then, after covering my hands back up with the cuffs of my shirt, I help Isabella to pull Anthony to his feet. Hooking the boy's arm over my shoulder, I pant, "Where's Felix?'

'History.'

'History!' I try to look at her but Anthony's bristly skull is in the way. 'You didn't - kill him, did you?'

'No, silly,' she says with a chuckle. 'I'm not a murderer. But I did hex the rotter. He'll be pooping slugs for a week.'

Totally and utterly bewildered, I nod stupidly, my thoughts fuzzy, my skull full of cotton wool. Then, for want of anything better to do, I help Isabella to drag Anthony from the big top.

'Did you just say 'pooping slugs'? I ask her

hazily.

'Yes,' she says. So coolly, I might just as well have asked her to pass the salt.

'So you must be a...'

'Witch. Yes.'

'I see,' I say slowly.

'Do you? Honestly?'

'No,' I confess. 'Not even a tiny, tiny bit.'

We tow the comatosed bully by the remnants of a bench, now a hill of cinders and blackened screws.

'Yesterday,' I begin, 'in the library, the pencil...'

'My back-up wand,' Isabella interrupts me. 'I'm supposed to keep it in my sock but I keep forgetting.'

'Am I a wizard then?' I ask her.

'No. Well, yes.' She sighs. 'Sort of.'

'Sort of,' I echo her. 'Sort of yes or sort of no?'

'Did Bus try to kill Anthony?'

'Yes.'

'But he didn't.'

'No. I stopped him.' I frown. 'Well, I think I did.'

'Then no, y' sort of not.'

With a 'TWANG!' a rope in the roof snaps and the flaming wall of the big top begins to sway and fold in.

'Hurry,' barks Isabella. 'Or we'll be burnt.'

Gritting my teeth, we stumble on. But foul, black smoke fills my lungs, sapping what little strength I have left. A flaming ladder thumps to the floor and shatters, blocking the way with splinters of glowing wood.

'What now?' I cry.

But, with a flick of her wand, Isabella sends the fiery shards scattering.

I will my curly-tipped feet to go faster, faster, FASTER! And, with burning timbers crashing down and sparks flying up, we stumble from the tent.

TOMORROW

Chapter 9

RISING FURY

THE NEXT MORNING, I SIT WITH ISABELLA ON THE graffiti-wrapped bench in the shadow of the bicycle shed. It is 8.27 and the school bell will soon ring. I got here at 8.05; Isabella 8.19, but so far, but for a fleeting 'Hello, Mop. Feeling better?' to which I answered 'Hello, Isabella. No, I'm not.'

she's not spoken a word to me. Not a word. To be honest, I don't think she - or I - know where to begin.

Yesterday evening, after we dropped Anthony on a stretcher - I dropped him anyway, with a very satisfying thud - I slipped off, grabbed my cardigan and iPod from the clowns' tent and simply left. I did not even stop to say goodbye to Isabella. I returned home at 9.57 and got to see thirty-seven seconds of Star Trek.

The next morning, Billy Smart's Circus was the top story in the newspapers. 'TOWERING INFERNO' trumpeted the Trotswood Express and, lower down, squeezed between 'MAN HIT BY FLYING PORK CHOP' and 'LORRY CARRYING APRICOTS TIPS OVER. JAM ON MOTORWAY', a tiny report on how Bus, the elephant, was discovered in the Spar munching on a bag of frozen carrots.

That, I thought, is what happens when you don't stock Star Trek comics.

On seeing all the terrifying reports of crying children and scorched candyfloss, Dad got very upset; so upset, he dripped hot coffee on his foot. But I kept my wits and threw my bowl of Sugar Puffs over him. After wiping up the milky mess, he insisted on checking me for burns. Then, after plastering up my three blistered fingers, he insisted I do not go to school today. But I told him, 'I'm not missing my Thursday 10 o'clock trumpet lesson with Mr Clench.' I then instructed him to sew the buttons back on my cardigan.

As Isabella and I sit there in the sun, not knowing what to say or even how to say it, I spot

I Think I Murdered Miss

Anthony on the street trying to disentangle himself and a long, wooden crutch from the passenger side of a rusty Ford Focus. Finally, he slams the door shut and, with the help of the crutch, he limps through the school gate and over to us.

'Wotcha,' he mutters.

'Hello,' chirrups Isabella.

He's still my enemy so I mutter and chirrup nothing. I simply nod.

'How's your foot?' Isabella asks him.

'Much better. They took me to hospital and a doctor there - I think she were Chinese - she fixed me up. She told me to keep off it for two weeks.' He snorts. 'As if!'

'Clever thinking,' says Isabella with a roll of her eyes.

'For a moron,' I add.

For a moment, Anthony just looks at me. I can tell he's dying to thump me, but, to be honest, I'm no longer bothered and I look stonily back at him.

Wedging the crutch in his other armpit, he rubs his bristly skull. 'Look, I er, just wanted to say - thanks, you know, for carrying me out of the tent. I don't remember too much but I remember you finding me and I remember being,' his eyes flit to me, 'dropped on the stretcher.'

'No problem,' tweets Isabella.

'No problem!' I growl. 'No problem! I MISSED STAR TREK!' I waggle my three bandaged fingers at him, further proof of the agony I suffered.

'Don't worry,' Isabella says comfortingly to

the startled Anthony. 'He's just being difficult.'

The bully sighs. 'Anyway, thanks Izzy. Thanks er, Simon.' Using his crutch, he begins to slowly swivel. But then, he stops. 'Did you know the circus elephant's name is Bus? It was in the Trotswood Express. Odd, don't you think?'

All of a sudden, I feel very hot and I unbutton my collar. Isabella, on the other hand, stays cool. 'Odd,' she says. 'Why?'

'Well, old Miss Belcher, she were hit by a bus after fighting with Nut, er - Simon here.' He looks to me, his eyes narrowing. "Then, the very next day, you told me you hoped I'd get hit by a bus too. Y' know, the elephant went crazy in the big top. If it'd trampled on me...'

'But it didn't, did it?' Isabella jumps in.

'No. No, it didn't. Still. Odd.' He shrugs, his

thinking power spent, and limps off.

Looking over at Isabella, I see she is chewing thoughtfully on her lower lip. 'Do you know who Mors is?' she suddenly asks me.

'He's the copper on TV.'

'No, not 'Morse', idiot. 'Mors.'

'Oh. Er, no.'

She grunts. 'Don't worry. Few do. But history is full of her. The Hebrews dubbed her the Destroyer and the Angel of the Abyss, the Romans, simply, Mors. It is written she kicks her way into the hovels of the poor and the towers of kings.'

'I still don't know who...'

'The Grim. Do you know who the Grim is, Mop?'

I snort. 'The Grim is just a silly monster. He's only in books and kids' films.'

'No, she's not.'

'She?'

Isabella dips her hand in her bag and pulls out a semi-demolished Snickers. 'I'm so hungry,' she mutters.

Do her parents ever feed her, I wonder. Or do her three brothers and her dog, Muffin, gobble up everything? 'You know, you remind me of a baby hippo. Chomp. Chomp. Chomp.'

She shrugs and chews off a colossal hunk. 'Sixteen years ago, the tomb of Khufu was discovered in Egypt...'

'Yes, I know.'

'How?'

'Er, history books? You know, ink, tiny letters. They form words.'

She balloons her toffee-filled cheeks. 'God, y'

such a nerd. Anyway, you won't know this. Under the mummy...'

'They never discovered the mummy,' I butt in.

She nods. 'Well, we did, and, under it, we discovered a scroll. On it, written in blood, were the words 'Ammit is with child. The world is doomed.' If you know who Khufu is, you'll know who Ammit is.'

I nod. 'She's the mythical demon of the underworld. A devil. She feeds on the unworthy.' Isabella gulps down another lump of the Snickers. 'You'd get on well,' I add.

'Ammit is just a different name for Grim or Destroyer or Mors.'

'And you think this evil demon had a child? You trust this 5,000 year old scroll?'

'The Sorcerers' Covern do. Sinjin Fury too.

They think the child grew up and had a child too and so on and so on. We hunted the history books trying to find them. We suspect the Roman Emperor, Nero. He fed children to dogs. Then, 500 years later, Attila the Hun...'

My chin hits my chest. 'You think I'm the descendent of...'

'No! No. We did. We - suspected. But not now.'

There is a low, rumbling growl. Hoping there's not going to be another thunder storm, I look up, but all I see is a passenger jet lazily circling the town.

'Why's it so low?' Isabella asks.

I shrug. Thankfully, it's not directly over us so there's no risk of plummeting poo. Not on me, anyway. Abruptly, the jet stops circling and veers off, flying north.

Swivelling on my bottom, I turn to Isabella. Her eyes, I see, look smudged like a panda's. I don't think she slept very well. 'So let me get this right. You thought I was the offspring of this demon, Mors.'

'Well, not directly; not your mum. But - yes, sort of.'

'Sort of. I see. But now you think I'm not.'

'Now we know you're not.'

'Why?'

'Well, we...'

'Who's 'we'?' I interrupt her. 'This Sorcerers' Covern?'

She sighs. 'No. My family. We met in the night. All seven of us.'

'Oh.' I nod, knowingly. Now I get why she looks so tired.

'To tell the truth, it's not my family. It's just a cover. so nobody suspects I'm, er...'

'Different?'

She shrugs. 'Yes. Different.'

'So your three brothers...'

'Not my brothers. They just - work with me.'

'And your mum and dad?'

'Not my mum and dad. A stroppy witch and a very old wizard. Awful cooks too; they burn everything. So I munch on toffee bars all day.'

'Your dog, then. Is your dog, Muffin, a dog?'

'No, she's a wolf.'

'Muffin, the wolf?' I ask her in astonishment.

'No, Ruger the wolf.'

I nod. 'Better.' A butterfly flutters in my belly. I never met her family and now I know why. Her family's not her family but a gang of magical secret agents. It's mind-boggling.

'Mop, if you were who we thought you were, Anthony'd be worm food by now, but he's not, so the danger's over. There's no Mors' blood in here.' She puts her finger to my chest. 'Sinjin Fury and his gofer, Felix, will no longer try to kidnap you.'

'Err, two-foot rule,' I remind her sternly.

'Oh, yes. Sorry.' She drops her hand to her knee. 'You know, I was sort of hoping we'd gotten by all this two foot gibberish.'

'It's not gibberish,' I tell her. 'It's a rule.'

She sighs and stuffs the rest of the Snickers in her mouth.

I think for a moment. 'But Miss Belcher...'

'She was just unlucky. You wished for her to be hit by a bus and a bus hit her. End of story. If you wished to win the lottery and you did, there'd still be no demon's blood in you. No magic.'

My brow knots in thought. 'And this - Sorcerers' Covern...'

'My boss. They tell me where to go, who to follow. Who knows where they'll send me next.'

'So y' going?'

'Yes, Mop. I'm going.' Scrunching up the Snicker's wrapper, she lobs it in the bin. 'I'm a Seeker. My job is to discover if this long lost offspring of Mors truly exists. Fury will not stop until he finds him. It's my job to find him first.'

'Or her,' I correct her.

She nods. 'Or her.'

The school bell rings but we ignore it and stay put. 'Why's this Fury-fellow so keen to find this person?' I ask her.

'Sinjin Fury's evil and evil feeds on power. The power to kill with a wish, well, it's simply too tempting for him to resist. Fury's so keen to find this person so he can put him,' her lips twitch, 'or her, to work.'

'I see. And Felix?'

'His little helper.' She snorts. 'He's scum. In it for the gold. Oh, and he's short too. Short men, never trust them. So, will you miss me?'

'I will miss correcting your grammar.'

She grins and blows a curl out of her eyes. 'Oh, stop it. Now I'm blushing.'

I try to think of the correct thing to say. 'You know, when chimps say goodbye, they kiss the other's chimp's bottom.'

She rolls her eyes. 'Honestly, Mop, the stuff

you know.'

'Just saying,'

'Well, if I ever do say cheerio to a chimp, I will try not to turn my back on him.'

'Very prudent," I tell her. With a wrinkled brow, I play with the newly-stitched top button on my cardigan. Still not everything adds up. 'Why me?'

'Sorry?'

'Why did you suspect me of being this long lost child of Mors? You moved here to Trotswood four months, three weeks and three days ago. Why? Did you suspect me even then? And, if you did, why did you?'

Interestingly, she begins to scratch the top of her skull with her index finger. Dad told me this is a sign of 'perplexity'; of not knowing the answer. Or not wishing to tell it. I shuffle down the bench a bit. He also told me it is a sign of nits.

'It's er,' she balloons her cheeks, 'complicated.'

'It's a good job I'm so intelligent then,' I retort.

The low rumbling is back and I look up. The jet, I see, is returning but now it is flying even lower and, if I'm not mistaken - I hardly ever am - it looks to be sort of twitching as if the pilot wants it to go a different way.

'What's the idiot playing at?' asks Isabella, jumping to her feet.

I lumber up too. 'I don't know. It's the Airbus 350. I can tell by the wings.'

'It's the Air-WHAT!?'

'The Airbus 3...' I stop, my mouth still open.

I Think I Murdered Miss

'Oh no.' I look over my shoulder to the school. The yard is now empty but for Anthony who is still hobbling his way over to the doors.

'Anthony,' murmurs Isabella. We begin to run. 'ANTHONY!'

The boy slowly turns but the growling motors of the jumbo jet pull his eyes up and left. In the closing seconds of his life, all Anthony sees is the petrified, conker-nosed face of the pilot battling the controls, then the A350 bellyflops onto his black, steely crewcut.

Hypnotised, we watch the jet slither over the grass, ploughing a deep cleft in the dirt. The port wing thumps the gym wall and snaps off, but the rest of it keeps rumbling on and on until, finally, with a screech of twisting metal, it stops, just short of the door to my French classroom.

Pity, really.

'My God,' mutters Isabella, turning to look at me. 'Mors' blood is in you.'

Before I can think of what to say, the door to the crumpled jet pops open and a slide uncurls from the bottom of it. We stand and watch the passengers slither to the grass. But for the odd cut brow and broken leg it looks as if nobody but Anthony was killed.

Everywhere, children and grown-ups run, yell and cry. And in this swirling throng of flaying hands and stumbling feet, I see a man. A man in a bowler hat with a matching black umbrella clutched in his fist. A man with a hanky peeping up from the top pocket of his stripy, buttoned-up jacket. A man who looks as if he's just left the office for the day.

I Think I Murdered Miss

With a twirl of his umbrella, he begins to stroll over to us; and, I think, from the look of his puckered up lips, he's whistling.

Isabella sees him too. 'Sinjin Fury,' she mutters, jitters distorting her words.

'No! Honestly?' I frown. No third eye. No wolf's teeth. Not a monster at all. 'He looks like a banker,' I tell her.

She turns to me, gripping hold of my cardigan so roughly, she rips off all three of the newly-sewn on buttons. 'Noooo!' I cry.

But Isabella, it seems, is in no mood for my funny ways. 'Run,' she tells me softly. 'Run and never stop. Trust nobody.'

'But my dad. I must...'

'No, not even him. I'm sorry, Mop, but Fury's no fool. He will think to look there.'

'This is nuts,' I protest. Fury is now only sixty feet away and still coming. 'I - I know Miss Belcher was hit by a bus,' I splutter, 'and Anthony too, sort of, but maybe they were just terribly unlucky. Two is just, well - two.'

'No, Mop. Not two. Three.'

'Three?' In spite of everything, I guffaw. 'Honestly, Isabella, your adding up frightens me.'

'GO!' She prods me in the chest. 'Sinjin Fury must not get his claws on you. Or it will be the end of everything. For everybody.'

'But...'

To shut me up, she pulls me to her chest and hugs me. 'To be honest,' she whispers, 'I think your two-foot rule sucks.' Then, she thrusts me away. 'Run!' she yells, brandishing her wand at me. 'Run or I will kill you myself.' Then, with a snarl, she turns to face the evil wizard.

Utterly bewildered, I lurch over to the school gate. But there, I skid to a stop. This is not the Star Trek way. I can't just desert this girl. She's my - my best buddy.

Stiffening my knees, I look over my shoulder only to see poor Isabella slump to the grass. She lay there, her right leg oddly bent, her cheek dripping blood. With a cowboy swagger, Fury strolls over to her and yanks her wand from her fist. Then, with a wolfish sneer, he snaps it in two.

Slowly, little by little, he looks up. I feel my legs turn to jelly and the thump, thump, thump in my chest almost stops. He has the sinister, tomb-like eyes of the Gorn.

'Where you going, Simon?' His mouth is oddly

still, but the words echo in my mind, low and gravelly. 'There's so much to do.' He grunts; a sort of bullish snort and his thin coppery lips twist up. 'A world to destroy.'

Horror creeps over my skin, throbs in my chest.

Then I do run.

I run.

And I run.

And I run.

I Think I Murdered Miss

THE DAYS AFTER

TOMORROW

Chapter 10

A STORM COMING

BY DAY, I TRY TO KEEP TO THE WOODS. IT'S MUCH
safer. Then, at night, I walk. I bundle up my few
bits and bobs - a toothbrush I discovered in a

bin under a dirty nappy and a jumper I snatched off a peg in the Nobody Inn - and plod on.

I walk for six hours, stopping only for food; often just plums off a tree or, if I'm lucky, the left overs of a Big Mac. Then, on I go, trying to get as far from Trotswood as I can.

I walk.

And I walk.

And I walk. Always wary of not putting my foot on a crack.

Two nights ago, I spotted my photograph in a newspaper. 'BOY MISSING' it bellowed to the unlistening world; and, just under it, a report from the jet crash. 'It's as if it had the devil in it,' the pilot told reporters, echoing the words of Jimmy, the bus driver.

I know Sinjin Fury's out there hunting for me,

stalking me like a tiger in the long grass. Every day, storm clouds scurry over the sun and I know he's not far away. So I keep on going. He must not find me. If I truly am the long lost offspring of this devil, Mors, if I truly can kill with a wish, who knows what horrifying things Fury wants me to do.

I often think of poor Isabella. Did Fury kill her that day in school or is she OK? Is she laying in a hospital bed or is she, this very second, trying to find me; help me?

I often think of Dad too. Poor Dad. He just lost Mum...

Mum!

Isabella told me 'three', not 'two'. Miss Belcher, Anthony, but who is the third person? She told me this Sorcerers' Covern tells her where to go and who to follow. She's a Seeker; her job, to find the son of Mors. But they sent her to Trotswood on the very day Mum passed away. Why? WHY? Unless...

Trudging up sleepy village streets and on the muddy banks of rivers, I often find myself dwelling on the blazing row I had with my mum on Christmas Eve and the terrible, terrible thing I wished Santa for.

Follow Simon on his exciting adventure in

DROWNING FISH

Coming Soon!

The Boy Who Piddled In His Grandad's Slippers

Words by Billy Bob Buttons   Drawings by Lorna Murphy

Printed by Amazon Italia Logistica S.r.l.
Torrazza Piemonte (TO), Italy